D0951562

THE PICKLE INDEX

THE PICKLE INDEX

ELI HOROWITZ

ILLUSTRATIONS BY IAN HUEBERT

FARRAR, STRAUS AND GIROUX

NEW YORK

Farrar, Straus and Giroux
18 West 18th Street, New York 10011

Library of Congress Cataloging-in-Publication Data
Horowitz, Eli.
   The pickle index : a novel / Eli Horowitz ; illustrated by Ian Huebert. —
First edition.
      pages   cm
   ISBN 978-0-374-53581-0 (paperback) — ISBN 978-0-374-71422-2
(e-book)
I. Huebert, Ian, illustrator.   II. Title.

PS3608.O7675 P53 2015
813'.6—dc23

                                                        2015010110

Designed by Eli Horowitz

1   3   5   7   9   10   8   6   4   2

For Caroline Fish and Augie Kunkel

DAY ONE

"WE GOT HIM."

by Yevgeny Pinkwater - The Daily Scrutinizer

The strike team spotted the compound from above, a pinwheel of menacing color amid the drab hills of our nation's fermented birthplace. Six female rangers parachuted through the humid darkness and then crept toward the compound, which was enshrouded in a ring of overlapping canvas sails, a counterraid strategy that rendered the team's shatterbolt equipment useless. The sails were adorned with strange occult patterns, portraits of large and/or hairy men, depictions of snarling hounds; whether these images were intended as dazzle camouflage or crude propaganda is still uncertain.

The team established a position just outside the largest tent, moving silently to elude the target's henchmen, a cadre of collaborators that mirrored his elusive swerves across the rural districts. A biothermal scanner revealed the heat signature of the target's breath, which appeared to be emanating from within a primitive wooden trunk. The team surrounded the tent while the shooter and her wingman entered through a flap in the front. Confirming the agency's intelligence, the suspect's inner sanctum was in a state of menacing squalor: An array of crude hand-smithed knives scattered upon an empty barrel. Reams of flash paper and explosive charges. Books on disappearance, on live burial, on mind control. Chains and restraints. Dog collars. Matching windbreakers.

The remainder of the team rushed the tent, assuming a three-horned assault formation around a crate marked *Wigs n Things*. They carefully removed the lid and trained their weapons on the charismatic hatemonger cowering within—now just a trembling man in a tattered white tuxedo, half-buried in human hair and oversize shoes.

That man is Zloty Kornblatt, the instigator, conspirator, and fomenter, who was apprehended by an elite preemption squad mere hours ago. Kornblatt and his troupe of disciples had been traveling throughout the Burford encampments for several months, a recruitment drive posing as theatrical gaiety. Even as simple theatrics, these "performances" would have been unlicensed and therefore illegal—but, of course, insufficient licensing was the least of Kornblatt's crimes, and theatrics were far from his true aim: mockery, destabilization, and anarchy, blurring the serious with the comical and the comical with the unintentional. Let Kornblatt's capture serve as an example to any others who would sass all that we hold dear.

Through his rabid dedication to anonymity, Kornblatt had evaded government surveillance for several years—until, like all men of low character, he became sloppy. Yesterday evening, at a solicitation rally for prospective foot soldiers, he overlooked the presence of one Clemford Moritz, undersecretary for Burford Region Cohesion Enhancement. Moritz, shocked by Kornblatt's lacerating personal attacks upon our Madame J (attacks so vicious and provocative that I am prohibited by law from relating them here, not that I'd want to anyway), filed a report in accordance with the new Transparency Initiative, instituted to ensure complete openness in all government–citizen interactions. Moritz's report was delivered to his semiregional oversecretary, who quickly informed his division's unanimity council, and so on, each bureau elevating the alert with admirable speed and thorough documentation. By dawn, Kornblatt was blubbering within the smooth walls of a mobile detention pod, bound for the Confinement Needle, where he shall remain (and blubber) until further notice.

In other news, Madame J today traveled from Destina to a cucumber farm in the northern territories, where she offered encouragement to the orphans working so hard to fill our nation's jars. The Madame was resplendent in satin fatigues, accented with an orange sash to match the oxygen masks of the children, and a mink cadet cap from which her golden bangs flowed like a waterfall. She toured the facilities on a moving platform and even walked among the children for a short time, favoring her right leg as she bore her wartime injury with grace and composure. In the crook of her arm she held Simeon, the cobalt Javanese octopus that has become our nation's most beloved invertebrate. A bearded assistant carrying a spray bottle of saline solution kept Simeon moist while Madame J distributed ration poppers and finger wipes to the children, who then performed an aria of gratitude.

"Some people call these children orphans," the Madame said in a press briefing later, gently stroking Simeon with a white-gloved hand. "But I don't see them that way. They are the children of our nation. I am, almost literally, the mother of all these unfortunate little people you see all around you. I understand what a grave responsibility this is. That is why I am here. I can think of no greater honor than to nurse these children as if I birthed them myself." Citizens are discouraged from envisioning the Prime Mother in the act of nursing, whether literal or metaphorical; nevertheless, our nation's gratitude for the nourishment of her milk (strictly metaphorical) is very real.

May your strivings today result in actionable and profitable outcomes.

RECIPE NAME

[Hollow Gherkins]

INGREDIENTS
[Cucumbers; cuke-mites; air]

INSTRUCTIONS

Zloty left us last night. No one saw him sneak away, no one heard him pack his tuxedo and hat and disappear down the muddy road, but we woke this morning to find an empty tent. We slowly assembled in the wreckage of his hasty departure, the scattered wigs and lolling scraps of canvas, testaments to his eagerness to finally escape our dead weight. I looked from face to face, expecting defensive rationalizations or indignant accusations, but mostly everyone just seemed tired. Dieter squeezed a tedfruit in a trembling fist. Marina kicked a rock into a puddle. "Maybe he just stepped out to buy us cinnamon buns?" Reuben said weakly, but no one replied. The tedfruit burst in Dieter's hand, showering me with pulp. He turned and walked back to his tent, and one by one so did everyone else, until it was just me standing there amid the wigs and canvas and mud, bits of tedfruit dripping into my eyes.

There were plenty of good reasons to leave, of course, but Zloty had ignored them all for so long, and with such good cheer. Which one finally pushed him over the edge? Was it our bickering, or our incompetence, or our bad personal aromas? Was it me?

I couldn't blame him for giving up on us. Our old tour circuit had dwindled to a Burford-Dupton-Grütn triangle, and then just an extended residency in Burford, home of the pickle collective, the summer pickle olympiad, and the region's largest fossilized pickle. In the old days, our route was actually a route—Burford and Dupton and Grütn, sure, but then on to Moylrad and then Tubuntsi and all the western villages. Once we even made it to Spagg. We used to be a real traveling circus, one that actually traveled and was a circus—I mean, one that actually entertained people, at least a little. At least sometimes. We had all of the real circus things, once. Clowns, a trapeze, roasted nuts in paper cones.

Then came the night of the National Puppetorium fire. It was never clear whether the arsonists were anti-administration or just antipuppet, but a week later we woke to find that the valley separating Destina from Burford had been intentionally flooded, creating the scenic DestBurf River, our nation's wettest waterway. Destina thrived, a gleaming city of fruit salad and ornamental lasers, while the rest of us were left on the far shore, stewing morosely alongside our cucumbers. The Index was launched sometime around then, a vibrant forum nurturing pride in our nation's traditional cuisine, or at least that's what we were told. (The Index also served to distract anyone who might wonder about the dwindling supply of *non*pickled foods, at least on our side of the river.) It all felt mildly absurd, but no one wanted to laugh at the wrong thing, and the enhanced public-amusement regulations included specific prohibitions against bow-tied animals and excessive guffaws. It would have been a difficult climate for even a top-notch circus—and we were far from top-notch.

So the clowns and trapeze and roasted nuts slowly fell away, lost to decay or incompetence or ennui, and we sank deeper and deeper into the sticky Burford mud, the lights of Destina pulsing from across the river. Still we managed to put on a show six days a week—not out of any persistence or idealism, but just because Zloty wouldn't let us quit. He'd rouse us each morning, bubbling with grandiose schemes for each night. Somehow we'd muddle through the day, grudgingly surrendering to one final show—and then the next morning it'd all happen again.

It seems crazy now, but I once thought I was surrounded by greatness. I thought maybe I could help. Somehow Zloty never stopped believing, and so neither did we, at least not entirely.

Until, sometime last night, he did.

*   *   *

Yesterday began the same as the day before, and the day before that: in the morning, like every morning, I walked into town with a stack of flyers, and that afternoon, like every afternoon, I returned to our clump of tents with the same stack. I've developed a less-is-more strategy for promotion and outreach, a reverse-salesmanship technique wherein I strive to display absolutely no interest in the people who walk past me in the square. It works about as well as you'd expect. Back in our salad days, when I was still a naive girl in a flowery dress, I'd bark bally like a pro. "More fun than a drunken toddler!" I'd shout, with a little vibrato in my voice. "Thrills and chills and spills and dills! Anything can happen, and it just might!"

Over the years, though, that last line became uncomfortably true—we had no idea what would actually happen each night. Like Dieter, if he wasn't sulking in his pup tent, might decide to eat the pallet of tedfruit he was supposed to lift. Kovacsz could lose interest in his chained-submersion act and try freestyling with a flare gun and a bungee cord, which is how we ended up with seven regulars in the audience instead of eight. Martin Van Buren has been known to squat in the ring, lift his mangy tail, and dump a steaming pod of shitballs right in the middle of Reuben's tragic mustache routine. Sure, Martin's a dog, but still it's a real spirit-breaker. Last night's show wasn't any better than usual, but it didn't seem any *worse*.

I guess Zloty just couldn't stand it anymore—couldn't stand us anymore.

He began the show in the center of the ring, standing tall in his ridiculous top hat with the burst seam at the back. I steadied the spotlight, trying to keep him centered in the makeshift cone of light as he twirled and bowed spastically at the crowd. "Ladies and gentlemen, seekers and sojourners," Zloty boomed. In the rickety bleachers, a scattering of Burfordians stirred to life: the Dorfelmeier twins, Breal the Cart Hag, Undersecretary Moritz, and the catatonic Mrs. Tralm and her beef-eating sons. "You have flocked from far and wide," he said, referring, I guess, to the cardboard encampment on the east side of town, "drawn like moths to a flame, lured by tales of feats so amazing they defy belief. Ladies and gentlemen, I am here to say: believe! The tales are true. The feats are imminent. Tonight you will see a man lift more than a man should lift! A juggling duo united by love and bowling pins! A beautiful assistant, assisting beautifully! And much, much more. But first, let us begin with Valentino, wrangler of jungle fury, and his mighty Martin . . . Van . . . Buren!"

Earlier that afternoon, Martin had caught a musk eel in the floodpipe and gnawed it to pieces before taking a long, sprawling nap in the sun, the heat of which baked the foul smell into his fur. A fresh musk eel smells bad enough, but a single whiff of sunbaked musk eel on dog fur could turn your liver to stone. Zloty had urged Valentino to take the night off because of the stench, but Val insisted that it was his right as a shareholder in the Carnument to take part. When he entered the tent, dragging Martin Van Buren behind him on a tattered nylon leash, the audience recoiled, gasping for breath.

"You are correct to gasp!" he proclaimed. "What you see before you is an animal on the verge. A primal creature capable of extreme carnage, held at bay only by the power of my mind." A hurled pickle exploded against the tent post, spattering Valentino's brow, but he continued unfazed. Martin cowered between his legs. "You see this, do you not?" he called out. "The beast is entirely under my sway. Were I not present to command this animal, each of your sad lives would be at risk." Martin sniffed the air for a moment, then daintily cacked up a pungent wad of musk eel. Zloty quickly hustled the pair offstage, applauding wildly.

"Wonderful job!" he said to Valentino. "The majestic terror of the animal world, et cetera!"

"But is that booing I hear?" said Valentino. "Do they not comprehend the delicate mastery, the bloodbath narrowly averted?"

"Booing? Just the opposite! They are chanting 'Martin Buuu-ren'—the ultimate homage," said Zloty. Valentino brightened, and Zloty hurried back into the lights.

Bruce and Sharon were next on the lineup, but the spotlight remained empty after Zloty's introduction. I ran backstage to find them furthering the argument that began sometime shortly before their wedding and then persisted long after their divorce, now consuming every waking moment, a boundless epic of interleaved grievance. The flavor of today's debate seemed to concern body hair—whose body, and whether too much or not enough, it wasn't clear. I shoved them through the curtains into the ring and they began whipping tedfruits at each other, each catching a prickly orb and hurling it back at the other in a single motion. Their juggling was flawless as always, a blur of whirling fruit, and the crowd stirred into something like applause. Bruce turned to bow, and Sharon seized the opportunity to pelt him with three tedfruits thrown from a single hand, which nailed him simultaneously in his face, chest, and niblets. He crumpled and let out a slow, mournful whine, and I dragged Sharon into the wings before he could retaliate.

Zloty rushed into the ring to announce Dieter, a mountain of rippling muscle who marched into the spotlight with an enormous tree stump nestled under one arm. He set the stump on the ground, gently, almost lovingly, though it must have weighed a couple hundred pounds. The audience leaned forward, eager to finally get their money's worth with a few verifiable Feats of Strength. Dieter squared his shoulders and bowed his head, summoning some deep reserve of will. He then squatted and reached out with both arms, almost as if he were grasping some invisible rounded shaft hovering in the air above the stump. The spectators collectively squinted, suspense blurring into confusion. What they didn't know but I did,

13

wincing in anticipation, was that he *was* grasping an invisible rounded shaft. Dieter had recently announced that he would be transitioning from his traditional strongman act into Continental mime theory—or, in his words, "the eternal poetry of the human form." The thing he was doing now was a routine he had just developed: "Chopping Down Tree, Lifting Heavy Trunk." It consisted of him pretending to chop down an imaginary tree, followed by him pretending to lift the imaginary trunk. The actual physical stump was Dieter's one concession to reality— "the animating spark," he claimed.

The crowd's confusion bled into boredom and then anger as Dieter again and again "swung" the "ax" into the "tree," his face contorting with effort, muscles slick with sweat. By the time of his hammy "Timber!" bit, the audience was openly heckling. Dieter tried to ignore it, but I could see his lip beginning to tremble. A family-size tub of sauerkraut exploded near his feet, and he ran for the wings. The crowd jeered his departure, and the old canvas tent grew muggy with sweat and smoke and accumulated resentment. The mood was dark, darkening.

And then Zloty emerged, wandering into the middle of the ring, entering the spotlight in a halo of dust and smoke. He held his hat close to his chest, his eyes bright and searching, like a child lost in a market square, separated from his mother. If it sounds maudlin, it was, but it was just enigmatic enough to perplex the regulars for a moment. Their boos subsided as Zloty crossed the stage, my spotlight lagging slightly behind. I winced yet again, knowing what was coming next: a seventeen-minute reenactment of the life of the herpetologist Etienne Stratford-Hicks, depicted via classical clownery—Zloty's passion project. (It's not that he didn't *care* whether the crowd was entertained or enraged; he just wasn't very good at telling the difference.) He was trying out the bit for the very first time, and these bumpkins were going to tear him to shreds.

Zloty paused by the popcorn machine, gathered himself, and then sprinted toward the center of the stage. He flung his arms wide and leapt into the spotlight—where he landed in the puddle of Martin's festering eel-barf, which I had forgotten to clean up. His foot went out from under him, sending him into a long chaotic slide that ended in a kind of inverted split, cushioned only by the pile of overripe tedfruit that still littered the stage. It looked like he might have torn himself in half, and the audience drew a quick breath.

Zloty slowly rolled onto his back, coughed twice, and sat up. A tedfruit skin hung from his forehead like stringy blond bangs. He sprang to his feet, as if it were all part of the act, and marched back to the center—where he promptly stubbed a toe on Dieter's massive stump. His barely contained scream came out sideways as a high-pitched squeal, and I thought he was going down again, but he somehow managed to limp a few steps to the right, hobbling like a drunken penguin. The musk eel vomit had left a dark stain on Zloty's white tuxedo, under the left arm and across his chest, thick black tendrils of half-digested eel parts. He saw the mess and began wiping it away with his right hand. Valentino, embarrassed by his partner's indiscretion, rushed out from backstage with a bottle of cleaning spray and began pumping it at the stain.

The tent was silent. The sight of Zloty—blond, limping Zloty with a glistening tentacled thing under his arm—struck some long-buried nerve deep inside us. We had seen this before, so many times. On our walls, in our slender billfolds, curling out of our scrollers. And now onstage, inadvertent and so grotesque that it would have been almost comical, if such a thing were permitted to be comical. No one moved.

Then there was a sound from high up in the bleachers. A sound so rarely heard during Zloty's routines that I needed a moment to recognize it for what it was: laughter. It was coming from Mrs. Tralm, still virtually motionless but now almost gasping, eyes crinkled. As her surprisingly delicate giggles filled the tent, her sons began to join her, the pitch of their cackles mirroring hers. Then the Dorfelmeier twins joined in, and Moritz, and soon the rest of them were laughing, too. It was as if the years of unspeakable absurdity had been sealed up and tucked away—and now the lid had come loose. Even I may have chuckled for a moment. Everyone did.

Everyone but Zloty. Determined to finish the performance, he smiled through the pain, brushing the pulpy bangs from his eyes, which sent the crowd into new peals of hysteria. Zloty now grinned more widely and hobbled to the center of the ring, still trying to wipe away the stain, which Valentino's frantic scrubbing had only made worse. He was aglow—injured and sticky and, of course, clueless, but the star of the show nevertheless. He bowed deeply, and the crowd applauded, sounding almost like an actual crowd. The tedfruit pulp slid off Zloty's bent head, and when he rose again he predictably stepped right onto it. His foot slipped, his arms flailed, and he went over backward in a twisting, spread-eagled slump. I killed the spotlight, and this time the laughter billowed out of the tent.

By morning, Zloty was gone.

DAY TWO

"AIRBORNE PUSTULES."

by Hank Hamper - The Daily Scrutinizer

Citizens flocked to the base of the Confinement Needle this morning to catch a glimpse of Zloty Kornblatt as he was wheeled from the security transport into the prison, where he has been assigned to the top floor, Cell 7, for his own safety. Destinians frantically shot hot-pics and first-takes of Kornblatt's steel body-cage as it rolled through the Needle's expansive lobby, while little girls popped poppers, showering the crowd with a tasty dust of mink sugar. Vendors sold pancetta-wrapped plover eggs in malted satchels, and Krover's Bakery sent a pastry owl into the crowd to distribute oven-warmed goat paws and cocoa peppers free of charge.

Despite the festive atmosphere, the air was rank with an unmistakable Kornblattery. The man was apprehended, yes, but his *ideas* remain, airborne pustules of mental infection, wafting along a gentle breeze of passivity. A figure like Zloty Kornblatt does not simply materialize out of the fermented mists, and his network of dedicated followers does not simply wither away in his absence. At this moment, highly trained disruptor cells lurk just a river's width from Destina, in Burford, our nation's spiritual pantry, a city of earthy folk living happy, brine-spattered lives. These humble people aren't distracted by Destina's insatiable appetite for novelty, the endless chase for *new* flavors, *delicious* foods, *fresh* vegetables. They don't have to worry about being first to discover the new treat of tomorrow; there, tomorrow is the same as today and yesterday, only slightly more vinegary. Yes, theirs is an innocent, authentic existence, uncluttered by the pleasant odors and dull administrative powers of our capital city.

That innocence, unfortunately, is like catnip to the cynical hatemongers, who stalk the parks and public squares with their pamphlets, demanding attendance at their seductive, outlandish conscription rallies. And when they run out of converts in Burford, who do you think they're headed for next?

Therefore, it is not sufficient for us citizens to merely disapprove of these disruptors; our actions must be *active*, and the responsibility falls upon each one of us. If you notice something, notify someone. If you suspect a neighbor, inspect a neighbor. Is it a crime to emit a loud honking sound when one sneezes? Of course not. Might a loud honking sneeze be a ruse to distract listeners from some simultaneous criminality? Maybe. Could be. I just don't know, and neither do you, and that's exactly my point: you don't need to *know*. Don't stop and wait and think—just report the sneeze (form 19.g.5, Observation of Nasal Noise) and let the specialists do their specialty.

I am not asking you to take direct action. (To those of you who have already taken direct action, perhaps even while reading this text, I do appreciate your spontaneity and stridence.) I ask only that you listen to your heart, an organ that cannot lie. If you suspect that a fellow citizen is failing to contribute to the Index, or consuming gloomy rhetoric, or sneezing oddly, or just doing anything peculiar or inelegant, please alert the relevant department(s). Only when we are working as a team can we stem this tide and ensure the safety of our children.

I'm speaking from experience on this one, folks. As you've surely noticed, your longtime host in this space, Mr. Yevgeny Pinkwater, a man of prodigious girth and luminous prose, no longer sits atop the byline. Just like the rest of you, I devoured Pinkwater's updates every morning. Never missed a word. Dreamed about someday, some way, adding my *own* voice to the *Scrüt*'s inky chorus. It was this intimate devotion to Pinkwater's column, however, that allowed me to observe certain unsanctioned iambic patterns in his subordinate clauses, possibly as some sort of rhythmic code to outside agitators. As much as it pained me, I reluctantly informed my local council of this shocking behavior, and they smoothly ousted the traitor late last night. Pinkwater's departure left a blankness on the scroll, and I feel privileged to help fill the void: Hank Hamper, at your service.

You too can do your part! You too have eyes, and ears, and hopeful hearts. And if your dreams happen to come true along the way? I call that icing on the Bundt cake of truth and justice—sweet, circular, and all-encompassing, just like our duty, just like our devotion.

But even the simple request to keep one's eyes open seems to be too much for some among us. Regrettably, it seems that a portion of our population responds only to jealousy and fear, rather than to our national ideals of verve, obedience, and pluck. Visions of secret lairs lit by single bulbs, contraband blueprints marked with ominous scrawled circles, dirty-booted storm troopers stomping up and down our farmwomen's hand-hewn wooden staircases—do we need these scenes to actually *happen* in order for us to believe that they are real? Yes, Zloty Kornblatt is now in jail. Yes, he is extremely unhappy, regretting each foolish step since his very first toddles, the long and crooked path that led inexorably to his current dank cell. But his cohorts are surely planning their counterstrike at this very moment, drunk with delusions of resistance, the cartoonish lure of heroism. They are out there, and they are among us.

Thus, this is no time to let down your guard. Vigilance is our responsibility, and vigilance is our reward: the dusky comings and goings of our citizens, the hushed murmur of our nation's private moments, the dainty clump of our farmwomen's own moccasins pattering up and down those wooden staircases as we lay our heads to rest each night. To observe your fellow countrymen is the truest form of affection. Bear witness.

In other news, Madame J yesterday prepared lunch for the residents of the Spelunkers' Reorientation Center, three hundred pale gentlemen recently rescued from a gas hole, where they'd been trapped for over a decade. "When I pass a flowering zucchini plant in the garden, my heart skips a beat," the Madame said, setting out an impressive array of finger foods for the dazed hole-dwelling men, whose pale skin was almost translucent, in stark contrast to the Madame's robust glow. "I hope you feel the same about these cornmeal-dusted squash fritters, and also please feel free to sample any of the three dipping sauces: fennel relish, fizzy ajvar, and dill-whip." The meal indeed appeared delicious, but to this reporter's eyes it couldn't hold a candle to the nourishment provided by the Madame's simple presence, the warmth of her attention, the sudden gleam of her ready smile. As she looked on, caressing Simeon's moist forehead, the lucky men dined as if they had not eaten in days.

We have reached the maximum-allotted space for news and information. May your children make responsible decisions about their reproductive organs and use them to create a new generation of dedicated professionals.

SOURCE CITIZEN

[Flora Bialy]

RANK

[19,731]

RECIPE NAME

[Brined Snouts]

INGREDIENTS

[Elderly hog (or other snouted beast); roasted fennel; tears]

INSTRUCTIONS

I woke early this morning, the faint light filtering through the holes in my canvas tent. I waited for Zloty's face to appear, bushy eyebrows arched, fetching me for our usual morning rounds. Those were always my favorite moments, I think—just the two of us, before the damp world reasserted itself. As we walked among the wheezing sleepers, he'd tell me stories of bizarre acts, grandiose plans for new tricks, lists of historical figures whose lives were overdue for clown-based reinterpretation. In those quiet mornings, it all seemed possibly possible. At each tent, Zloty would rustle the flap and then begin a long, gentle campaign of persuasion, flattering and teasing and prodding, whatever it took to get each performer to the breakfast table and reassemble our broken shards into something resembling a circus.

I lay there for a long time, motionless, the thin blanket tucked under my heels and around my shoulders. Eventually the holes turned bright as the morning sun pierced the tent, and still there was no Zloty. I could hear birds scrabbling in the dirt outside, and a creaking branch. By the time the dill horn blew I knew he hadn't returned, but I lingered for another slow breath, mummified under the blanket. As long as I stayed in my tent, the old life was still ours. It wasn't much of a life, but it was ours.

Eventually I opened the flap and stepped out into another Burford morning, gray and steamy. No sign of Zloty, but otherwise our camp was as usual: tilting tents, scattered trash, Martin Van Buren nosing through the dirt. I didn't know what else to do, so I collected Martin and the tattered flyers and set out for Gaal Square. The road to town from our haphazard clutch of tents is a spongy mess, probably because of the underground rain farms. If you're not careful, you can find yourself up to your knees in suck-mud. I bring Martin Van Buren on my flyering runs so that he can whimper for help if I get stuck, a thing that has happened eight times so far. Martin also has a small roofed cart you can strap to his back, which is convenient for stowing the flyers.

The ancient pages are as wrinkled and stained as everything else in our camp, but beneath the smudges the show actually looks pretty good. There's an etching of a mountainous strongman (that's Dieter, his bald head agleam) brooding inside a dark cloud while a woman tied to a post (Marina, the beautiful assistant) smiles calmly into a torrent of knives thrown by a masked desperado. A ferocious hound (Martin, in his younger, less incontinent days) rears up, snarling at its trainer (Valentino, glowering behind a whip-thin mustache), while a sexy duo (Sharon and Bruce, pre-divorce) juggles a full peck of peppers. And in the foreground is Zloty Kornblatt, his arms raised skyward, with an inscrutable grin on his face, like he knows something you don't. I think that smile is what drew us all in. We wanted to find out what he knew, to believe as he believed.

Before there even was an "us," there was just Zloty, a skinny boy scavenging for crusts of breadbread on the streets of Spagg. A boy too thin and hunger-sharp to be dreaming of circuses, much less sketching the circus's logo on barrel lids and sewing a big top from old diapers. But Zloty knew, right from the start, that the circus was his destiny. Or at least this is what he believed, and for Zloty there was never much difference between the two. Some would call it foolishness, soft-skulled dreamery, but we just called it Zloty. He lured us in, one by one—not with false promises, and certainly not with money. I guess it was just that smile, his vision of what could be. Which never quite *was*, of course, but it always seemed maybe possibly around the corner. He was our ringmaster, head clown (and then only clown, after the clown purge), pyrotechnics specialist, kraut chef, marital counselor, and janitorial coordinator. He painted our tents with colorful, overblown advertisements that even we were almost fooled by. He turned our strange obsessions, habits, and defects into skills, talents, and supernatural powers, feats to be illustrated on flyers and barked to eager crowds.

The crowds never appeared, but I still have the flyers, oily and crepe-thin, the ink faded and worried away. Circus tonight, step right up, etc. Come to Kornblatt's Multivalent Carnument, where the expected is improbable. Kornblatt's, where we promise nothing and deliver double. Price of admission is two redheads and a cat's eye or you can trade us a chicken duster or a smokepoot.

(We could really use a smokepoot, actually.)

In the center of Gaal Square is the Burford Bureau of Public Works, a shingled structure with a bright blue door. Each afternoon I stop there on the way back to camp to renew our public-amusement license. Undersecretary Moritz sits in a tiny swivel chair in a little vestibule at the end of a long, dark hallway. Above him is a framed painting of Madame J. You can see the dusty outline of another frame that used to hang there, which held an old photo, taken before the uprising, of three men standing around a thresher, smiling into the harsh sunlight. They were burly, large-hearted men who looked like they'd been born with a bag of tedfruit seed in their hands. The first time we came through Burford, I asked Moritz if the men still lived in town—just mindless small talk to charm the local officials. He winced and said something about the weather. The next day, when I came back to have our license renewed, the photo was gone, replaced by the portrait of Madame J with the spike through her leg, fighting off the insurgent hordes. I didn't say anything. It's easier to just not say anything.

Today I submit the 77.r.3 (Declaration of Comedic Intentions) and try to leave before a friendly conversation can break out, but Moritz is too fast. He attends every show, always sitting on the topmost bleacher with a bag of cricket hash, never applauding or hissing, just slowly crunching the hash into oblivion. He might be our biggest fan.

"You still want a license?" he says, biting his lip. "Without Zloty?" I guess news travels fast in a town where absolutely nothing happens.

"Well, he might be coming back, right?" I say. "Maybe he's just"—I swallow hard—"getting cinnamon buns?"

"Cinnamon buns . . . yes, maybe so," Moritz says queasily, and hands me the license. "Need anything else?" he asks, brightening. "Perhaps a refill of scrollpaper? The penalties for an unstocked scrolltray have recently been intensified, and anyway there are some wonderful new designs for autumn: Parchment, Simeon On The Go, Simeon With Kittens, Monuments—"

"I'll take a roll of plain, please," I say.

"Plain? Really?" he says. His eyes narrow. "You are opposed to our nation's monuments?"

"Oh, monuments!" I quickly reply. "I thought you said . . ." I trail off, too weary to continue the charade. "Yes, monuments, that, please."

"Wonderful choice," he says. "Wonderful. I find that the monuments provide a stirring backdrop for the Pickle Index: our nation's first, best, and only forum for citizen-to-citizen fermentation-recipe exchange," he recites. "Why, it's virtually required reading for the modern gourmand!"

"I thought it was *literally* required. Legally."

"Well, yes, literally also," he says. "A recipe each night, original or forwarded, from each licensed scroller. Basement Gherks, Kelp Rompers, Sloppy Cheddar Dills—a literary smorgasbord, with new treats every day!"

For better or worse, that's a dill I'll never receive—our little scroller has been broken for months now. No morning news, no shared kraut recipes, no exciting brine tips passed among my hungry countrymen. The machine can still post outgoing snacks, presumably—at least, the buttons still light up, the page still slithers in, and it makes those fuzzy beeps when I punch a random number. Back when the machine worked, I'd do my duty as quickly as possible, just forwarding whatever scrolled out first. I'd watch the recipes bounce from scroller to scroller to scroller, and I'd imagine the happy families on the other end, gathering at overflowing tables, living normal family lives.

Then our inker busted, which meant I had to somehow create new dishes of my own. It was deeply depressing, of course, but the alternative was a visit from Moritz or worse, so I've been diligently scribbling out actual recipes, semiplausible slaws and whatnot. Sometimes I even picture those happy families raising their glasses to toast my ingenious creations and eloquent instructions—not that anyone ever reads past the ingredients, if they even make it that far. And with Zloty gone, it all seems more pointless than ever. Thus, apparently, my dishes have now devolved into these little notes, sad boring diaries of each sad boring day—recipes for despair; serving size: one. Please don't ask me why, or where I imagine them going. A fairy godmother? Zloty, wherever he is? Call it desperation, call it loneliness, call it mutated hope. I close my eyes and poke some numbers and try to forget about the whole thing as quickly as possible—it's all too pathetic to even speculate.

I dumped the scrollpaper in Martin's roofed cart and trudged back to the camp. As we came around the bend in the swampy road I saw two figures up ahead—a woman in a spangled cloak and an old man bent over a breathing apparatus. The woman was waving her arms and shouting, and the man seemed to be shrinking away.

"Marina," I called, dragging Martin Van Buren behind me through the muck. "Really?"

"Help," the old man said, wheezing into the fluted end of the breathing machine, his whole head bent to the ground, one eye cocked up at us. "She said she's going to stab me."

"I said nothing of the sort," Marina said, flicking her wrist at the man, who jerked back in fear. "I said I'd pay him to chuck some daggers in my general direction, and then I asked him if he'd want to *take a stab at it*. It should've been obvious that I was making a pun." Marina's specialty was assisting: smiling bravely into a hurricane of thrown knives, standing motionless as flaming hoops whizzed overhead, gesturing seductively at various apparati. But anyone with weapons expertise had been drafted into the prophylactic defense squadrons, and few had returned. Now Marina hung around Kornblatt's circus searching for someone to assist. Sometimes Zloty would let her wheel out his wig crate, but I could tell that only fueled her yearning. So she wanders the streets of Burford, looking in vain for a partner. The old man with the breather is a new low.

"Why are you even bothering?" I said, dragging her away from the gasping old man. "There's no show tonight, not without Zloty."

"No show? Wait till Zloty hears you say that. I'm sure he's around here somewhere. He loves us too much to leave! In fact, I bet he's watching us right now." She looked suspiciously down at Martin Van Buren, as if Zloty was somehow nestled within his bony ribs.

"People leave, Marina. That's what they do."

She rolled her eyes and followed me back to the camp. As we passed the ticket booth Martin caught sight of Valentino carefully arranging a bowl of scavenged scraps. He lurched off toward the bowl, toppling the roofed cart and sending the flyers up in a wild plume.

"Oh, my precious chicken finger," Valentino said, crushing Martin Van Buren to his chest and giving him a squealing sideways kiss. "You were gone too long. Yes you were." He looked up at me. "Every time you return, I expect you to be missing limbs. How is it that you are not destroyed by my brazen little hellhound?"

I looked down at Martin, who was panting desperately. "I guess I'm just lucky."

"For now, I suppose." Valentino squinted into the distance. "One day he'll turn on you. He will rear up and tear into your flesh, and before you know it you will be on the ground, bleeding in torrents, and the last thing you see in this world will be the gnawed remains of yourself strewn out on the grass."

It wouldn't be the worst way to go—nibbled to a pulp by a mangy half-breed in a field outside Burford. Everyone else in the group loathed this place, but something about it felt right to me, like this was where we were meant to wither and fade. It had a certain disfigured charm, a glum drabness that I found soothing. The main street consisted of a handful of shacks, a shabby open lot where ratty women sold ratty tubers on ratty blankets, and an old awning-covered pig trough that served as the local bar and grill. No one clung to fruitless hopes. No one talked about Destina. This was where we belonged.

"Make sure to bring an extra blood-mop to the ring

tonight," Valentino said cheerfully. "Martin seems especially feisty." The dog shook out a morose belch.

"Tonight?" I said. "You, too? Without Zloty?"

"Oh, he'll be here any minute," said Valentino. "Zloty's always here. Just get it started. Maybe Kovacsz will help with the lights."

"Kovacsz?" I said, turning slowly toward his tent. "Helping?" I peeked through the flap and saw Kovacsz reclining on his cot, flipping through a cosmetology magazine. His hair was parted neatly down the middle, the two wings cascading down his scalp in lustrous black waves. He was wearing his satin singlet, though he hadn't actually performed in weeks; he wouldn't even leave his tent without a special onslaught of Zloty's adulation and bribery. At one point he had been our star attraction, the closest thing we had to a draw. His signature move was to fold himself up into a ceramic vase that was then dropped by a crane into a glass tube filled with snakes; *CarnyWatch* called his escape from the Knot of Mambas "painfully arousing." He could also slip out of a burning tub of peanut butter and dig his way through three feet of hard-packed sand. One time I saw him pick a rusty padlock using only his tongue.

Kornblatt had poached him from Baron Chepachet's Hippodrome of Wonders back in the early days. No one knew how much he had paid Kovacsz, but we were sure it was a lot—nobody left Baron Chepachet's troupe just for the heck of it. It wasn't until later that we found out

Chepachet was a finicky sadist who forced Kovacsz to sleep in a steel vault at the bottom of a mine shaft, just to remind him that there were still things he couldn't escape. Zloty had liberated him, but traces of that dark shaft lingered.

I rustled the flap. "Kovacsz?" I said.

"Kovacsz," he answered, "means nothing. An empty construct. Is Zloty back? I only negotiate with Zloty."

"Zloty is . . . busy. Look, you go out there, you put the chains on, you get in the tank. You remove the chains, you get out of the tank. Ten minutes tops. You can't do this?"

"I can do this, yes. But the question I am all the time asking: Why?"

"Because that's what the people come for. To see you escape from the Barrel of Doom."

"And I do escape. Obviously. I am not going to go up there onstage and die, am I? They come to see me escape, and I escape. Tada, I continue to exist. Doesn't it all seem a little circular? A bit futile? The one thing that is expected is the one thing that occurs. If I were to melt into mustard or procreate with a badger—those, I grant you, would be surprising. But mere survival? That, unfortunately, is the default status of our drab march. Thus, why can't I skip the ropes and the chains and instead simply jump ahead to the ending? Do you realize how the metal links chafe against my thighs? Why can't I just be Kovacsz? Kovacsz the Living. Kovacsz the Left Alone."

"You *are* Kovacsz. You *are* living. And we're all very

glad about that. But the point is . . ." I paused, trying to remember what the point was.

"Zloty understands my predicament. Bring me Zloty and we shall discuss. Furthermore, I may be developing an allergy to the brackish barrel-water. Either that or it's these tedfruit fritters. Do we have anything else to eat?"

We didn't, and the show was about to begin. I sprinted to Zloty's tent, carefully keeping my heart clear of anything even resembling a hope, and yet still I was crushed all over again to find the disarray exactly as we'd left it—crumpled canvas, scattered wigs, and no Zloty. I rummaged through an overturned trunk and found his backup tux, which I quickly put on straight over my clothes. I looked more like a space-suited pigeon than a ringmaster, but there was no time for standards.

I hurried to the big top, where our seven regulars were already scattered through the splintery bleachers. To my right, there was Mrs. Tralm, her sons Ishmael and Bodie, and Undersecretary Moritz; to the left, I could see Breal and the Dorfelmeier sisters, as well as what appeared to be a small family of raccoons feasting on a tattered bag of popcorn from back when we bothered to pop the popcorn. "Ladies and gentlemen," I began, "do we have a show for you tonight." My proclamation sounded more like a question, so I scrambled for an answer. "We do, yes. A series of performances, unpredictable in nature, outcome, and quantity. Possible juggling, definite bickering. A man who is capable of lifting large objects, both real and imagined. A dog minding its owner." The Dorfelmeiers spat on the floor and Breal gnashed her wooden tooth against her ivory tooth. "But first, let me introduce: Reuben Montalban, master of the . . . well, he can probably describe it better. Reuben Montalban!" I extended my arm and did a sort of backward shuffle offstage.

Reuben strode into the middle of the ring, chest first. "You have no doubt seen some wondrous things in your lifetime," he said, waving his hand into the spotlit haze. "I regret to inform you that tonight all of those moments will be rendered inert in comparison to the feat of epidermal biology I am about to reveal to you." He tugged at the fabric of his pants, settling into a weight lifter's squat. "Look closely at my face as I concentrate," he said, and then assumed an expression of extreme discomfort. "Observe my freshly shaven visage, bare as a baby's belly. But now, under these harsh lights, you will witness a stonecold miracle at work. I will grow a full beard of healthy human hair through the follicles in my face." He went silent and shut his eyes tightly, teeth clenched. The Tralm boys whistled and spat, and one of them threw a mollusk shell at Reuben, which glanced off his thigh.

"Look now!" Reuben shouted, rubbing his chin. "Can you not see the stubble that is growing there?"

Breal got up and left. I hoped she wouldn't be asking for her smokepoot back.

Reuben squinted out of one eye. "Come back tomorrow morning," he challenged them. "Come back and see that I will have a full, thick, healthy beard. I will invite you to tug on it to verify its authenticity!"

"I have a dentist's appointment tomorrow," said Ishmael Tralm.

"Also, what, it's just a beard?" said the elder Dorfelmeier, Sabrina. "I mean, who doesn't have one of those? Or even several?"

I hustled Reuben offstage before she could begin to disrobe. He sat down on a crate. "I don't understand," he said. "A full beard in under twelve hours! It's really quite remarkable."

"Quite, yes," I said halfheartedly. "They just don't get it."

"I'd rather they got it," he said, sighing. His cheeks were already growing dark with stubble.

I left him to his gloom and shoved Sharon and Bruce onstage. With no Zloty to mediate a brief détente, they didn't even bring anything to juggle—Sharon just began flirting with Undersecretary Moritz, while Bruce pretended not to notice and talked loudly to no one in particular about Sharon's "musty caverns."

Next Valentino and Martin Van Buren ran through their little thing—mostly Valentino shouting commands and hissing dramatically while Martin creaked and farted. Bodie Tralm began making theatrical snore noises, which soon transitioned into genuine snores, and then Martin himself dozed off. It was all too boring and sad to watch, so I didn't. If Zloty was here, he'd be . . . I didn't know what, but he'd be doing *something*, utterly convinced that the show could be saved, that the show had never been better. Zloty wasn't here, though. I was. Lonely, cranky Flora, whispering silent nothings to nobody. And what *I* decided to do was poke at the grubby floor and hope it'd all be over soon.

When I looked up from the pile of rocks I was carefully arranging with my foot, Valentino had gathered the sleeping Martin in his arms and was hobbling off the stage, which was the cue, sort of, to start Dieter's entrance music, a slow, syncopated rhythm I banged out on two rusty oil drums. Dieter stepped into the spotlight, wearing only a sarong of red burlap, nothing in his hands.

"Announce me," he whispered.

"Where are your props?" I hissed back. "You're not going to smash *anything*? Or at least lift something?"

"That's over. This is me now—pure gestural expressionism, no more gimmicks or distractions. No smashing."

"No smashing?"

Dieter didn't answer, just took a deep breath, laced his fingers together, and closed his eyes.

"Okay, then," I said, swallowing hard. "Okay. Ladies and gentlemen, I present to you Dieter, Destroyer of Worlds, who tonight will be, well, pretending to do some stuff, I guess?" Dieter opened one eye and shot me a hurt look, brow furrowed.

I patted my hands together a few times, simulating

applause, but the sound was quickly drowned out by a chorus of boos. Sabrina Dorfelmeier doubled over and began spanking her naked buttock. Her sister brandished a dill in each fist, cursing loudly. Dieter sneered at them and turned to walk offstage. In place of a farewell bow, he gloomily kicked at the rotting timber that served as our tent's central post. The post crumbled and then split, and the tent wilted like a wet tissue. Everything went black and silent for what seemed like a very long time. I could hear the muffled voices of the Dorfelmeiers as they struggled to find their way to an exit in the labyrinth of bunched canvas. Then I heard Bruce's voice, farther away, blaming Sharon for the collapse. Martin Van Buren whimpered. The rest were quiet.

"Dieter," I shouted into the heavy cloth, but no one answered. It felt like I was the only person in the world; no matter how loudly I shouted, no one would ever be able to hear me. So I curled up and shut my eyes tight, hoping I would fall asleep and awake to find the tent standing and everybody safe, everybody home, everything back the way it was.

DAY THREE

"QUICK, EFFECTIVE, AND USUALLY BLOODLESS."

by Hank Hamper - The Daily Scrutinizer

Crowds swarmed the streets of Destina shortly after dawn for Nibbles & Bites, the city's annual festival of snacks and snacking. The day's events began with the traditional foraging competition in Tejaratchi Square, where contestants hunted for drain nettles, snumgum pollen, and scrap metal shavings, which were then collected into an enormous black cauldron, an homage to the nourishing "stew-stews" of yesteryear. Interns tended the stew-stew as it simmered throughout the day, allowing the piquant, earthy flavors to ripen and intertwine, whereupon the cauldron was tipped into the sewer and scoured clean by a swarm of rat tongues. Citizens then rushed to line up alongside a decommissioned methane transport, which was rumored to be offering an innovative trout-based gelée. After several hours of waiting, the amassed gourmands became antsy and began rocking the tanker back and forth, attempting to signal their desire for the gelée within, at which point the vehicle toppled over and burst into flames (apparently still containing methane, not the rumored gelée) (which, hot tip, I heard is actually being served via a repurposed soap dispenser under the West Spagg Thruway).

Mingling almost unnoticed amid the festive herds was Madame J herself, shielded only by Chief Grunfeld and the swarthy spray-bearer, who kept Simeon slick and moist in a silvery cloud. The crowds, alerted by a local journalist's giddy yelp, rushed to surround the Madame, pleading for photos or, ideally, a song. She repeatedly demurred, but the citizens were insatiable, until a cloud of intensely realistic smoke burst across the stage and a dozen white doves fluttered from the persimmon sleeves of her blouse. Madame J then led the masses in a rousing medley of our national anthems, accompanied on the xylophone by the winner of this year's talent search, nine-year-old Lars Bobrow. The prepubescent goof didn't know how lucky he had it, mere steps away from Madame's robust lungs, those tapping toes, that mouth wide with song, attacking and sustaining with the precision of an opera star. As she gracefully sculpted each syllable, the audience could not be blamed for wondering what it might be like to have those crimson lips gently graze one's earlobe, singing softly or perhaps whispering. Cooing, even.

Following the performance, invigorated citizens

thronged the stage, waving plastic spoons and soiled napkins. Chief Grunfeld stepped to the swarm. "I sense a lingering hunger within you all," he said, raising his hand skyward. "A hunger for *justice*. And today you may drop the *i* and call me 'Chef,' because I am here to tell you that justice will be served. I am here to announce that *tomorrow*"—his hand moved higher—"we will *begin*"—the hand became a fist—"the *trial* of Zloty Korn"—the fist thrust boldly into the sky—"*-blatt!*" The crowd roared its approval, and Grunfeld continued through the din. "If Kornblatt is somehow able to prove himself innocent of these charges, let that be displayed for all citizens in the marble-walled temple to our nation's highest ideals. If, however, he is guilty, let those smooth yellow walls echo the tones of truth and retribution in a buttery chorus of justice."

Scrüt reporters ventured out into the crowd in the aftermath of Grunfeld's announcement. Commented one onlooker, "When he was caught, I felt good. That was, like, days ago. I miss that feeling. Maybe I'll feel that way again if he's squashed underneath something big." The representative citizen stomped his foot symbolically, then added: "Or ate by a vampire whale."

I'm with you, brother! A mere locked cell isn't quite enough for this guy. Look, is Kornblatt *himself* dangerous? We can't be certain (but probably). Does he *represent* danger? Without a doubt. The crime of threat is the crime of fear, and is not this crime even worse than violence itself? Violence is finite. It is measurable and unambiguous. It has the dignity to announce itself, to define itself. Fear, however, is boundless, indiscriminate, wanton. If Zloty Kornblatt was man enough to carry out the attacks he was no doubt planning in his moist Burford lair, then at least our citizens could have confronted real pain, and eventually found real closure. But in his cowardice and passivity, Kornblatt did absolutely nothing—and this was the worst thing he could have done.

There are those who think this entire process is silly, those who say a man like Kornblatt doesn't deserve a trial, doesn't deserve justice. They, like the representative citizen we quoted earlier, would be content if our leaders simply crushed or otherwise eradicated him and let that be that. I am tempted to agree—but then we would be no better than the man himself. No, we must scrupulously observe the required procedures set down in our founding documents, procedures which ensure justice via their precision and formality.

That said, if it so happens that the jury sentences Kornblatt to death, an execution has been scheduled for next Tuesday at the Termination Field, mere steps from his current accommodations in the Confinement Needle. Please be sure to register for the mandatory ticket lottery well in advance of the deadline in order to avoid late fees, restrictions, and possible jail time, and be advised that standard execution-day traffic rerouting will be in effect. In keeping with our nation's democratic ideals, the method of execution will be determined by popular vote.

Submit your suggestions via scroller or loud conversation, and don't be afraid to get creative! Sure, we all know a good hanging can be satisfying, and it certainly is quick, effective, and usually bloodless. But sometimes a traditional hanging leaves one with the aftertaste of a punishment not necessarily fitting the crime. Where's the symbolism? As opposed to, say, a gaze of swamp raccoons. How many swamp raccoons would it take to chew a man to death? Don't you sort of want to find out? Would we have to first slather him in peanut butter? These are the sorts of decisions our leaders empower you, the freethinking citizens of Destina, and also you Burfordites, Duptonians, and Spaghetts too, to decide for yourselves, using the wisdom, verve, and handsomeness for which you are so justly known.

Of course, who knows if there'll even *be* an execution. If there isn't—which is technically possible!—we'll just have to save the raccoons for later. And do not worry: your submissions will still become the exclusive intellectual property of the administration, to be considered for use in future executions and/or theatrical productions.

The numbers are still being tabulated, but it looks as if Madame J's vocal medley will become the most-scrolled event in Destina's history, flooding the Pickle Index with more than six hundred Madame-themed recipes. In fact, a single dish (Sweet MJ's Skewered Cuke-Scoops) was forwarded to *over 83 percent* of all citizens on the Index. Rumor has it that a sizable chunk of those forwards came from a certain humble scribe . . . and rumor, as usual, is spot-on. I can't help it—I'm a J-Head through and through!

We have reached the maximum-allotted space for news and information. May your will to succeed keep you strong during the day and vigilant through the turbulent seas of sleep. May Madame J's smile radiate upon me in my dreams, and perhaps even a morning someday.

SOURCE CITIZEN
[Flora Bialy]

RANK
[7831]

RECIPE NAME

[Hundred-Year Shrimp]

INGREDIENTS

[Pungent dill; pungent shrimp; raw vinegar; no neighbors]

INSTRUCTIONS

My father ran a gas farm in the Brosian hill country. At the start of each season, a military airship would hover over the fueling circle, which was the signal for my father to wheel a cramble pole out to the middle of the circle. The airship would connect to the pole and then puff up like a loaf of breadbread. Those were good days. My sisters and I would run out to see the massive ships lurching in the sky above. They often had messages painted on their surfaces—advertisements for the future. I remember one painting that showed a group of children sprinting across a wheat field holding shovels and pink silk ribbons, grinning in their turquoise jumpsuits. Below the image were the words "Fresher Fields in Five Years!" There was a young girl in the foreground doing a cartwheel, and she looked just like me—so much so that I thought it actually *was* me, the way that children think the whole world has its eyes trained on them. But my sisters said it, too. I was convinced that this was no coincidence, and—although I never told anybody this—I felt like I'd been chosen to lead the nation in this great movement toward bounty and comfort. It was my ship-proclaimed destiny. I didn't have a shovel or a silk ribbon, but I had this feeling in my gut that great things were going to happen.

The next year the same airship docked, looking sunbleached and battered, and the painting, though peeling away in flakes, still claimed that the freshness was five years away. And the next year, while we drank cloudy brine and punched one another in the stomach to stop the hunger pangs, we were still five years away from the new age. Five years on, after the antibreakfast initiatives, I understood that we would forever be trailing five years behind the dream of prosperity. I saw that I was not the chosen one. There was no chosen one. My purpose in the world, which once seemed so clear and crisp, had fallen away, and in its place was just the glacial creep of the hard days ahead.

Then one day Undersecretary Moritz visited the farm with two men in coveralls who didn't speak but just measured things. The height requirements for cramble poles had changed, apparently, and a citizen had reported my father's violation. My father sighed, looked at my sisters and me, and agreed to join the military. He was sent to fight in the Gurdash Preemption as a burrow trooper, but his tunnel flooded and all we got was a pair of dirty goggles and his teeth in a metal tin. My sisters ran off with a pair of twin nut-shellers, and I was left alone on a leaky gas farm with a bunch of shadows and ghosts. The decades to come stretched out before me, a long flat road to nowhere. I was only at the start, but already I could see the whole journey.

And then Zloty's circus passed through the village downvalley from the farm. I was out prodding dirt mounds on the tuber hill when I saw the brightly colored tents in the distance, peeking through the dead tree line. It just didn't make any sense—something like that in a place like this. I stared at the tents for a long time. I still had three more mounds to prod until I filled my self-imposed quota of prodded dirt mounds, but instead I dropped my dirt-prod right where I stood and went to investigate.

The show was just beginning when I arrived. Zloty stood in the center of the ring, his arms outstretched, tracing circles in the air to indicate the boundlessness of the wonders we were soon to witness. He used words like *intrepid* and *spellbound* and *liability waiver*. He said we were *privileged* to *witness* such *feats*. Had I ever really witnessed anything before? I searched my memories, but mostly it was just a whole bunch of ordinary seeing. On the farm, there was only the work and how the work got done. You looked at the dirt mounds, you looked at your hands, splinter-rich from the dirt-prod, and then you went to bed. But to *witness* something—to become an accomplice just by watching—that was something else.

The show itself was not, by any traditional standards, a success. Martin Van Buren slept through his entire performance, and a disappointed customer poured gasoline into the vinegar tub. By the grand finale the bleachers were almost empty. But I hardly noticed—I was entranced. I stayed until the end, when half the troupe came out to take a bow to scattered, anemic applause. And I stayed to watch Reuben push a wide broom across the dirt floor and into a pile in the corner. And while they dismantled the ring and packed up the lights, I curled into a wooden crate filled with novelty wigs and buried myself deep inside. If I wasn't chosen, I would choose. I'm a performer now, I thought, and I felt the netting of a wig settle into place just above my ears. I thought about my dirt-prod still lying next to those three mounds, and then I fell asleep.

When I woke the crate was open and I was inside a much smaller, smellier tent. The only light came from a tepid fire in a steel pipe. Zloty sat at a folding desk with a book in his hand, and when I stirred he glanced at me. "Our little friend is awake," he said. He was a slender, long-fingered man with a wispy beard and a sharp mustache. He gave me a sly smile.

There was a rustling sound and Dieter came into

view behind Kornblatt. He was the largest man I had ever seen—the width of a two-horse carriage, with a face as broad and sharp as a steam shovel. He leaned in close to examine me.

"We should send her back to Brosi. She can't be trusted," Dieter said, looking away from me with disgust and pity.

"You think she's stowed herself away in my wig case to keep tabs on us," Kornblatt said, turning just a degree to wink at me.

"Just like Kueve," Dieter said.

"Kueve? Kueve was a thief! He joined only for the free cotton candy. Cried himself to sleep each night. Some spy he was."

"He was a spy."

"Well," said Kornblatt, "if this little girl is a spy, then I welcome her, because we have absolutely nothing to hide. Kornblatt's Multivalent Carnument is a fully licensed and authorized organization, Party-approved and operational for seven full harvests. If she finds a single infraction, even one, I'll eat your hand raw, Dieter."

"Eat your own hand," the giant said, and stumbled out through the flaps.

The tent fell silent again and Kornblatt returned to his book. In the dim firelight I could barely make out the title of the volume: *Techniques for Staged Immolation*. The battered binding looked as if it had survived multiple floods, or maybe a bar fight.

I tried to apologize for stowing away in his wig crate, for the trouble it was going to be to take me all the way back to Brosi, but Zloty just gave me that crooked smile, the one I would come to know so well, and continued reading, making notes in the margins and occasionally chuckling to himself. The fire slowly dwindled to glowing coals, and I sank into the crate and fell back asleep.

I woke to the sound of rainfall. I was still in the crate, but the tent was gone from around me. I turned and saw Martin Van Buren peeing sloshily onto a stack of folded popcorn bags. Beyond him, a slender man in a singlet was unfurling a striped canvas sheet. He noticed me staring. "If you're going to watch me unfurl," Kovacsz said, "you might as well do the unfurling yourself and learn that it is not worth watching." He tossed the canvas bundle at me and walked off toward the big top, which was just being hoisted into place. Dieter tugged on a thick rope tied to the center post while the others advised or heckled. I picked up the canvas and started unfurling.

Somehow I ended up manning the smoke machine that night, and then helped dismantle the bleachers afterward. When they were all packed and ready, I stood off to the side, trying to figure out how I was going to get home to Brosi, but Zloty threw me the key to the caravanner. "Let's get moving," he said, hoisting his crate into the back. "It's a long ride to Klobouk, with plenty of suck-mud on the way, and Kovacsz says driving makes him queasy."

And so I drove, first to Klobouk and then Maynep and Tront and on to Ploly. Zloty put me to work chipping the guano from the bat cages, and then I got to tote the scroller from town to town, and then I was also ripping tickets, and then one day Zloty gathered everyone together and declared I had been promoted to junior ringmaster. My heart flared for a moment, but I quickly tamped it back down; there was a vat of Reuben's beard tonic that needed mixing, not to mention Kovacsz's dietary restrictions and Martin's incontinence, and also showtime was just three hours away and Dieter had outgrown his performance cloak. Anyway, ringmastering was for ringmasters, and I still had the bat cages to clean. "You are so good with that shovel," Zloty would say, tousling my hair. "You are a true master. I would not deprive you of an opportunity to display your talents." Sometimes I thought about the farm, the dirt-prod, the three unfinished mounds, but never for very long—there were so many bat cages.

That was six years ago. I think. The seasons here range from damp to moist to humid, so it's not always easy to notice the transitions. One winter we were forced to trade the bats for tedfruit and extra jars, so at least there was no more guano to shovel, but still I'm doing a little of everything, and a lot of most. I'm no longer a little girl, and I'm no longer such a sucker for enchantment. I used to dream of someday standing in the center of the ring myself, mesmerizing a hushed throng of ladies and gentlemen, spinning acts into feats. Now mostly I dream of a waterproof blanket, and mostly I keep my mouth shut.

This morning I was awoken by Kovacsz sneezing theatrically outside my pup tent. That was his way of asking me to get up and cook breakfast.

I grabbed the sieve, waded out into the creek, and panned for whipfish. When I had scooped enough I brought them back and dumped them into a skillet, poured some potato oil on them, and sprinkled in a handful of crushed elephant grass. I liked watching the whipfish go from translucent to golden brown, and the smell of them cooking got everyone up out of bed.

One by one they appeared at the long folding table where we ate our meals. No one mentioned last night's mishaps. No one mentioned Zloty. Bruce somehow got a blade of elephant grass lodged in his nose-hair, but Sharon seemed too weary to even mock him. The only sound was the crunching of the whipfish. Then the whipfish were all gone, and still we sat. No one spoke. The sky was gray and the ground was brown.

"Maybe he's out recruiting a knife thrower," Marina said. "Or a lady-cutter-in-half."

"Maybe he's off on a tedwine bender, stained with ditch mud and his own vomit," said Kovacsz.

"Maybe he found a better circus?" I said quietly. The

others squinted at me, confused. Then we heard a rustling sound outside.

"Wonderful news today, friends, eh?" It was Undersecretary Moritz, craning his neck into the tent.

There was a long pause, until silence became more painful than the alternative. "News?" I finally said.

"You must be joking, my dear friends!" he said, taking the opportunity to slip into the tent. His head grazed the canvas, showering everyone with the soaked-in rainwater. "You don't read the *Scrutinizer*?"

I had used the monuments for kindling last night, not that the scroller worked anyway. We stared back at Moritz blankly.

"Friends, they have announced that Zloty's trial will begin tomorrow. A chance to get all the facts on the table!" he said brightly, slapping his palm on our own table, which teetered in response. "The divine gears of justice and all that."

"A trial?" said Reuben. "Why a trial? What about the cinnamon buns?"

"I believe the official charge is antagonistic fomentation," answered Moritz, "with a side of gratuitous slapstickery."

"Fomentation? Antagonistic? Zloty?"

"Well, his performance three nights ago . . . I hate to put a label on art, and I do indeed believe Zloty to be an artist, of course—but some ham-fisted officials may have simplistically inferred certain resonances between Zloty's performance and a certain lady, a certain beatific leader of ours, and thus he has been residing in the Confinement Needle." I felt a pang of something like relief—he hadn't left us, at least not on purpose—but that was quickly swamped by a flood of sick fear.

"He's been in *prison*?" said Reuben, clutching his thick trunk of beard. "And now there will be a trial? And you call that a good thing?"

"We all know how those trials go," said Marina, rising from her seat. "We all know how they end."

Moritz smiled nervously and then choked it down. "Look, I am a loyal admirer of Zloty's work—of all of yours! But we need to trust in the process. It's out of my hands now."

"What do you mean 'now'?" snapped Kovacsz. "When was it in your hands?"

"Well, I mean, never," he stammered. "Hands? Who said anything about hands? What do hands have to do with this?" He chuckled loudly, holding his palms in front of him like exotic fruit. "It's possible that I might have chatted about that wonderful performance—that's just me, I'm a chatter, everyone knows that. I love to share, I can't help it."

"And who did you happen to share this with?"

"Well, my memory, you know"—he gestured toward his head, fluttering his fingers—"but, if I had to guess, well, animals mostly, the leaves, the river, possibly Regional Administrator Pupnt, some sheep, my diary—"

Now we were all standing. I felt my lips twisting into a snarl.

"Pupnt?" Sharon said, gripping a fork tightly.

"Just to make conversation. And, you know, to fulfill my civic responsibility to memorialize the activities of the greater Burford populace."

"You mean to rat on us," hissed Bruce.

"Words!" Moritz squealed, giggling frantically. "So many words! Let's not debate semantics. Unfortunately, Pupnt, that ravenous buzzard, claimed the information as his own and passed it along to the Central Liaison, who of course are always eager to pump up their prevention numbers, and from there the Unanimity policies took over. It was mere data collection, I assure you—nothing personal! Simply following appropriate procedures. Without appropriate procedures, what are we? Who would decide who would decide?"

"But—you mean the slips and the tedfruit and the eel barf?" said Reuben. "Those were just accidents!"

"Accidental comedy is perhaps even more dangerous than the intentional kind. We can't have people laughing at just *whatever*, can we? I mean, how would we know what's funny? Zloty's stumbles were no laughing matter—or, I mean, they *were* a laughing matter, but the *matter* of the laughs was—"

"And you come here to tell us this?" Marina said through her teeth, approaching Moritz slowly. "As if we are your friends?"

"Well," Moritz said, backing up to the entrance of the tent, "I do like to think of you as friends, yes, which is why I came here to tell you."

"I will show you friendship, you verminous brine-sponge," Kovacsz said, pushing the table out of his way, sending our empty plates crashing to the floor.

Valentino stood in the scattered whipfish husks, clutching Martin's leash in his fist. "Shall I set my hound upon him?" he asked. "Are we prepared to sop the blood from our dining tent?"

We surrounded Moritz and Dieter scooped him up in a single hand. Moritz flailed like an inverted cockroach above Dieter's head. "Should we smash him?" Dieter asked.

Bruce pushed his way toward Dieter, lugging a wooden barrel. "Let's pickle the bastard."

Dieter dropped Moritz headfirst into the barrel and Bruce slammed down the lid.

"Friends, friends!" Moritz gurgled from inside. "This is not how I envisioned our encounter!"

Dieter tipped the barrel on its side and rolled it through the entrance to the tent. "Goodbye, friend," he said, giving the barrel a gentle kick. It tumbled down the hill toward the stream, until it hit a rock on the bank and shattered, sending Moritz into the pool of mud.

We stood outside the tent, watching his tiny figure splash and moan.

"This is bad," Marina said. "The things they will do to Zloty."

"The cruelty of their methods," Reuben said, "is matched only by their creativity."

"I heard they filled a woman with corn kernels and then left her in the sun till she popped," said Sharon.

"I heard one boy was forced to eat his own teeth," said Bruce. "Then they made him smell his own nose."

"A man like Zloty," Valentino said, "does not deserve such a treatment."

"Without him, I would be a peanut whore in Juke Valley," said Marina. "They would have stapled a tail on me and thrown nuts for me to dodge and made me talk like a baby nutmouse. Zloty saved me from this fate. Only he believed in my abilities."

"I was growing novelty mustaches for pennies on the streets of Ploly when he found me," said Reuben. "He taught me to harness my powers. He made me an artist."

"I loathe all men equally," Kovacsz said. "But Zloty, I admit, was slightly more tolerable than most."

Moritz stood in the muck at the stream's edge, brushing reeds from his sleeves, looking away from us to maintain a shadow of dignity. Valentino took a kerchief from his breast pocket and dabbed his eyes. Martin Van Buren chewed on the rubbery head of a whipfish. Zloty wasn't coming home. He was gone for good, and we were nothing without him. I'd go back to Brosi, back to the farm. Finish prodding those dirt mounds, find some new mounds to prod, repeat, the end.

"We will go get him," Dieter said, high in the back of

his throat, his voice catching on the words. "We will go to the place where they are keeping him, and we will get him out of there."

Everyone went silent. I glanced at Kovacsz, ready for a derisive snort, but his face showed the same icy resolve. Sharon was nodding slowly, her mouth a thin line. Valentino clenched his kerchief in a white fist.

"So we are in agreement, then," Dieter said.

Reuben stepped forward and put his hand out. "For Zloty." I reached to join him, but everyone else stared at his hand blankly. "Group clump," he said. "You guys never did a group clump?" Kovacsz wrinkled his forehead and looked away. Reuben's hand slowly returned to his side.

"We'll need food and water," Dieter said. "Nothing you can't carry. Let's go." He turned and started walking down the hill. We scrambled to follow him, picking up whatever seemed useful, which, it turned out, was a tin pail, two dried tedfruits, a suitcase full of breadbread, and Reuben's collection of famous nails from history. I scooped up the scroller, and we were off. We descended into the valley and then walked alongside the creek, the Destina skyline glowing in the hazy distance. It felt right. It felt like a plan.

DAY FOUR

"MORTAL, RUMPLED, AND GLUM."

by Hank Hamper - The Daily Scrutinizer

The trial of Zloty Kornblatt began this morning, with popular anticipation rising to a fever pitch in the twenty-four hours since Chief Grunfeld's snacklamation. The hushed assembly sat shoulder to shoulder on marble bleachers beneath the expansive mural of Madame J encountering a silverback gorilla, its wide eyes transfixed by the single ostrich feather held aloft in the Madame's naked hand. Imagine, dear readers, what it must have been like to be that gorilla. Imagine what it might be like to be that feather, gripped for a moment in those slender fingers. The things I might tell her, were I a talking feather in her grasp, or perhaps not even a feather at all, but just myself, adrift in the pools of her azure eyes.

At that moment Madame J herself entered the courtroom. She limped down the aisle unannounced, without security, accompanied only by her sallow, bearded assistant, the Simeon-moisturizer. This reporter was surprised and—well, let's leave it at "surprised"—to observe that not only was the ankly, sunken-eyed assistant *not* carrying a spray bottle, which is literally the sole reason for his being in Madame's presence, but that Simeon himself was nowhere to be seen. Now, of course, our Madame has been known to leave Simeon in the palace from time to time. She didn't bring him on her peace mission to the Gurdash Steppe, certainly, because of the unforgiving climate. And of course you remember, readers, that Simeon did not accompany our greatest lady on her visit to Jackal Run due to his fear of jackals. (But then what was the hirsute lackey doing there, cozying up to the blond beacon? Were they just, like, hanging out?)

These questions were pushed aside for later consideration, as the court came to order with the ceremonial Crumpling of the Brochure, symbolizing our nation's rejection of judgmental outsiders. A trio of local tweens then came forward to recite the Bill of Freedoms and Reasonable Constraints in its entirety, and finally Judge Dobler was lowered to the dais, where he donned his crimson sash, signifying that the trial was officially under way.

(I mean, isn't the guy technically her employee? Wouldn't that be weird? Not that there even is a "that"— of course there isn't.)

The prosecution opened their presentation with simple data: A three-dimensional mindmap demonstrating how a single Kornblattian utterance, overheard by a single passerby (in this simulation, a bare-necked dairy-maid), could potentially infect a city of thousands within a week. A bar graph comparing harvest cycles, citizens' relative susceptibility to corrupt thoughts and ideas, and attendance levels at Kornblatt's solicitation events. Judge Dobler was especially impressed with the prosecution's furiously detailed, accurately scented quarter-scale diorama of Kornblatt's lair, with bearded, unwashed toddlers standing in for Kornblatt's accomplices.

The lights then dimmed, and the lead attorney announced the introduction of an evidentiary reenactment. Out waddled local funnyman Chet Choochy, wearing a top hat and a white tuxedo, Kornblatt's infamous, iconic uniform. All eyes—jury and journalists alike—flitted from Choochy to his subject and back. Aside from quick glimpses through the bars of the mobile cell, few citizens had actually seen Kornblatt before today. Now, in the clean fluorescence of the courtroom, where a blemish is a crater, he cowered beneath the wide brim of his battered hat, a grotesque contrast to the sharp cerulean jumpsuit provided to him (free of charge) by the security concierge. Stripped of his cohorts and disguises, Kornblatt appeared mortal, rumpled, and glum.

Choochy portrayed a typical day in the life of a rural barnstormer: trudging into town, submitting his performative application to Judge Dobler, and gloomily erecting a big top in the witness stand. The moment he stepped inside the tent, however, a chilling giggle slithered from his throat, and his eyes burned with a terrifying glow. Even his fake mustache seemed to gain an extra curl. With the jury box as his rapt audience, Choochy re-created the swirling terror of Kornblatt's recruitment rallies: the elaborate rhetoric, the menacing props, the wild gesticulations. He railed and raged, he ranted and panted. "And now," he hissed, "for my grand finale!" He raised his index finger to the ceiling, paused dramatically—and then, with a sly smile, let loose a low rippling parcel of gas from his hindquarters. The assembled onlookers burst into relieved laughter.

"Objection," Kornblatt shouted, struggling to be heard over the guffaws. "Objection!"

"Objection?" said Judge Dobler, wiping a tear from his eye. "On what grounds?"

The wiry shadowman stood up in the defendant's box (not permitted in the courtroom), trembling (also not permitted) in his blue onesie and crumpled hat. "On grounds of hamminess, your honor! Fart jokes? He's plucking the low-hanging fruit. He's *scavenging* for *fallen* fruit. He's pandering!"

"Mr. Kornblatt, you'll have your chance to speak tomorrow. For now, just sit back and try to enjoy the show. Choochy is one of our finest edutainers, fully certified and demographically beloved—you should be honored!"

Choochy quickly resumed his performance, mincing around the courtroom, propositioning young boys with a slide whistle, and at one point pretending to pick his nose with Judge Dobler's gavel. This reporter has never seen an audience actually die from laughter, but a few jurors really did seem on the verge of cardiac distress as they cackled in their reserved box.

The smiles, however, were quickly inverted by the introduction of the prosecution's next item: overnight surveillance photos of Kornblatt's erstwhile compound. The encampment, once a grimly efficient hive of activity, now lies dormant, fallow. All residents have departed, leaving behind only a pile of whipfish bones, remnants of some ritualistic sacrifice; notably *not* left behind were any high-grade explosives, suggesting that such explosives may be on their persons. This, in turn, suggests that the now-mobile band of violent behemoths, dogfighting deviants, nihilistic lock-pickers, and tightly clad jugglers may be headed toward Destina, plotting to disrupt the orderly flow of justice.

Faced with this intel, government officials have swiftly erected a security checkpoint at the Burford entrance to the DestBurf River Span, in order to ensure that Kornblatt receives the fair trial he deserves. Readers, take notice: All travelers seeking access to the central district must be prepared to present their identification papers. Only registered residents of Destina will be permitted into the city, and all other travelers will be detained until completion of Kornblatt's trial and subsequent (potential) punishment, after which dates will be set for the travelers' own trials and subsequent (potential) punishments.

Groups of unkempt oddballs attempting to just stroll into Destina and muck things up will be rebuffed with extreme prejudice. Travelers carrying unusual snacks will have those snacks confiscated and heavily sampled. Citizens of the central district are encouraged to limit their travels outside the city, both to avoid long lines at the checkpoints and to remain at a safe distance from antagonistic influences roaming Burford and beyond.

The courtroom buzzed with speculation upon Kornblatt's fate. Would he be force-fed wolf crabs until they ate him from the inside out? Would he be killed by a thousand paper cuts in the Death From 1,000 Paper Cuts chamber? The excitement was palpable as the audience departed the courtroom. Madame J and the misting mister waited until everyone else had filed out before making their exit. Despite the stately hall's wide doorways, the two appeared to be standing in strangely close proximity. My stomach felt funny.

SOURCE CITIZEN

[Flora Bialy]

RANK

[1026]

RECIPE NAME

[Cuke-Fudge Dippin' Stix]

INGREDIENTS

[Fudge; cukes; dippin' stix]

INSTRUCTIONS

We followed the creek until it merged with the stream, and then the stream until we found the road that led to Destina. We walked quickly, piecing our way along the rutted path. The sky above was orange and purple and brown, never black, and I chose to see this as a sign of hope, rather than off-gassing from the fermentation vats that dotted the horizon. No one spoke, but I knew they felt it, too. We would walk until we reached the city.

The details beyond that were still fuzzy. We knew Zloty was in prison. We knew we had to get him out. We hadn't yet put together a plan for the parts in between, but I think we all assumed there would be some paperwork we could fill out, some form 73e, Petition for

Release (Comical Misunderstanding). If we had to, we'd even find a way to talk to Madame J herself, explain how the whole thing was just a mistake, a series of silly accidents. All of that would come later, though. For the moment, our path was clear, one foot in front of another until we reached the prison walls. We were, as Reuben said multiple times per mile, unstoppable.

Until we crested the dusty hills above the DestBurf River and . . . stopped. The bridge gleamed and twinkled, arching high across the thick brown water, but the entrance was blocked by two pudgy men in blue uniforms standing in front of a long, low-slung structure that saddled the ramp. Great lengths of cyclone fencing spilled off both ends. The guards slouched at the gate, smoking curved pipes and fanning themselves lazily with thick clipboards.

"Is this a welcome kiosk?" Valentino asked, pulling on Martin Van Buren's leash to draw him closer. "For a welcome kiosk, it does not look very welcoming." The dog, which had been preoccupied with the carcass of a dustmouse, whimpered as Valentino wound the leash around his hand.

"Maybe it's some sort of bake sale?" said Reuben. "A very well-guarded bake sale? Because the muffins are so delicious?"

Marina squinted at the men in the distance. "Let's go talk to them, I guess. Or, I mean, I will talk to them. Nobody else say anything, okay?"

We walked slowly down the bank to the building. A conveyor belt disappeared into a hatch in the side, just below a small window. Through the window we saw a head like a hand ax, gray and droopy-eyed, framed by an elaborate kerchief.

"Papers," the head said, in a voice that you'd expect to come from a head shaped like an ax.

"Papers?" said Marina. "Just to stroll across our nation's most scenic span?"

The inspector gave her a cool stare. "A scenic span which crosses into the city of Destina. Which, pursuant to this morning's 14.f.3, is now restricted to Destina residents only. Kornblattian invaders are to be repulsed or, ideally, pulverized. You are all, I trust, residents of Destina?"

"Um," said Marina, "yes?"

"Very well, then," said the inspector. His eyes seemed to droop a bit more, like they might slide off his face entirely. "Place your identification papers in the slot below, and your luggage on that belt." He pointed at the bread-bread trunk with his pencil and drew an imaginary line to the conveyor.

"And then we go through?"

"And then," he continued, "I will check your names against the list."

"The list?"

The man gestured behind him, toward the back of the shed, where we saw an elaborate machine that looked like the inside of a piano, each taut wire festooned with hundreds of small cards, each with a name written on it in neat script. "And assuming the names on the list match the names on your papers, you'll be on your way."

"And if they don't match?" Valentino asked. Marina turned and scowled at him.

"If they *don't* match," the man said, tapping the pencil's eraser against his chin, "I'll have to file the standard 424.b."

"Ah, the 424.b," Marina said, gripping Valentino's forearm tightly. "Of course."

"But what's the 424.b?" Valentino asked, half-squealing as Marina dug her fingers into his flesh.

The man scanned our faces carefully. "424.b: Permission to Insert Offenders into Vertical Well, Downward Orientation. A highly effective sequestration method for outside infiltrators, I find."

"Without a doubt!" Marina said, shoving Valentino toward Dieter, who backed away. "What better treatment for outside infiltrators? I can't think of one. Not even the 918.j would really keep out the riffraff quite so well."

Squinting, the inspector mouthed "918.j" and began to page through a large, gold-leaf book on the counter.

"Did I say 918.j? I meant, um— Right, allow me a moment to locate our papers. We're so used to living in the city and never having to present our papers that they're deeply tucked away, in a place where we seldom look for them."

The man watched us as we backed away from the window, smiling idiotically. We scurried to the overgrown banks and slipped into the shade of a spindly willow. I felt the mud seeping through the holes in my tattered shoes.

"Well," said Reuben, "at least we have a clear plan."

"Clear?" said Kovacsz. "How are you defining clear?"

"Only city residents are permitted through the checkpoint," Reuben said. "Thus, we must act as city residents do. The look, the speech. We must *become* city residents!"

"And the list?" Kovacsz said. "The one with the names of all the actual residents? The one they'll compare our names against, shortly after confiscating our bags and shortly before throwing us down a well?"

"Oh. That portion of the plan is not yet entirely clear, perhaps."

"Kovacsz," said Marina, stepping forward.

"Whatever it is, the answer is no."

"You can fit yourself into extremely small spaces, can you not?"

"I've already told you no."

"No you can't?"

"No, I can, but no, I won't."

"And we have this trunk of breadbread here."

"Breadbread. Only the most explosive of the edible grains, the cause of countless fatalities each harvest. Nothing you could say would persuade me to interact with that trunk."

"And, if you were to squeeze yourself alongside the

loaves, we could send the trunk through the conveyor belt and stall the guards while you add our names to the list."

"Such a simple and elegant plan," Kovacsz snorted.

"It actually did seem rather simple to me as I described it," Marina said.

"I, too, felt it was very clear and comprehensive," Reuben added.

"You are completely out of your cheese shop on this one. All of you."

Marina looked down at the trunk. "Is it too small for you?"

"Jesu has not yet created a space too small for me, unfortunately. But that's not the point. I have told you how dangerous even the crumbs of those loaves can be. Our days may be gray, humid drudgery, but still I do not wish to meet my end surrounded by yeast and idiots. Also, have I mentioned my allergies to the slats of the trunk itself? My thighs puff up like a fire newt in heat."

Marina was already on her knees, releasing the trunk's clasps.

"Apparently you're not hearing what I'm saying. I'm not going to risk my life for you people—we are mere coworkers, and hardly even that! I'm afraid I must decline. I decline. I decline. I decline!"

Marina took a Kovacsz-size bushel of breadbread out of the trunk. "Kovacsz," Bruce said, cracking his knuckles, "we all know you are the star. You have skills and abilities the rest of us would kill for. You were a center-ring attraction in Baron Chepatchet's Hippodrome of Wonders, even before the equine pox. But none of that mattered when you were crying yourself to sleep at the bottom of Chepatchet's mine shaft. No one cared about your skills and abilities then, and no one cared about you. No one except Zloty. You needed him, and he didn't fail you. And now he needs you."

Kovacsz looked hard at the ground. "So?"

"So," Dieter said, placing his meaty palm on Kovacsz's head, "you'll get in the damned box and get us through the damned checkpoint."

"All right, all right. But if this breadbread explodes, my blood will be on your hands."

"It'll probably be all over us, actually," Marina said.

Kovacsz looked out into the middle distance, eyes losing focus. He jerked his right shoulder forward, dislocating it completely so that his arm dangled over his chest, elbow out. He paused and made the same jerking motion again and his other arm cocked into place in front of him. He tucked his hands into his armpits and crouched. He began breathing quickly, and with each breath his hips spread, allowing him to throw his legs behind his head. I had witnessed this transformation nightly from my shadowy spot in the wings, but to see it here, in the flat daylight and scrubby grass, was astounding. Within moments, what remained of Kovacsz had the face of a man and the shape of a box. Dieter lifted him into the trunk and Marina shut the lid and fastened the clasps.

"How is he getting out of that thing?" Reuben asked.

"Magician doesn't give away his secrets," we heard from the crate, Kovacsz's voice muffled by the dense loaves of breadbread. Dieter hefted the trunk onto his shoulder.

"What if they don't let in dogs?" Valentino whispered, even though we were still a good hundred yards away from the checkpoint.

"We'll get the dog through," Marina said.

"But I fear what will happen if they try to separate me from Martin Van Buren. He will retaliate, and the carnage that will result . . ."

"No one is getting separated from anyone," Marina said. "Now, let's try to look like some plausible Destinians. Reuben, shave off that beard and fluff up your mustache. Flora, try not to make your face like that." I pushed my cheeks into something resembling a smile. "Bruce, wrap this scarf around your neck."

"Maybe he should try wrapping it around his whole face," added Sharon. "We're trying to fool the guards, not nauseate them."

"Maybe Sharon should have a snack first," Bruce said. "You know how she gets when she's peckish. We're trying to fool the guards, not eat them."

"Stop it, both of you!" hissed Marina. "We need to focus. Only say things Destina people would say. Do things they do. Now come on!" We emerged through the branches of the willow and started back up the ramp to the checkpoint window.

"Greetings, my good fellow!" chirped Marina when we arrived. "We are ready to return to Destina, our dear home!"

"I know," said the droopy-eyed inspector. "You were just here like two minutes ago. Bags on the conveyor, identification papers in the slot."

Dieter dumped the trunk onto the moving platform. I cringed, but no explosion followed, just a near-silent string of yeasty obscenities. "Of course, our papers," Marina said quickly, putting her arm around Reuben. "Honey, could you be a snuggledumps and dig out those pesky documents?"

Reuben stood at attention, eyes wide. "But of course, my dear darling," he said. "I will surely procure the documents of which you request. Please allow me a moment to initiate the aforementioned procural. Darling." He began rummaging through an old gunnysack that Marina had rigged into a sort of handbag.

"Do not delay," said the inspector. "There are dignitaries coming through for the trial and I will make sure the bridge is clear for them one way or another." Over his shoulder we saw the trunk slide off the conveyor at the back of the shed. One of the clasps came slowly undone, levitating as if by magic. I bit my lip, then regained my air of casual urbanity, whatever that meant—for me, apparently a dazed half-smile atop a lobotomized slouch.

"This will only take a moment," said Marina, who had now adopted a strange, operatic lilt, presumably her

Destinian accent, though I was pretty sure she had never actually been to Destina. "We secure our papers deep within our luggage, to protect them from these Burford folk. Their handicrafts can be quite charming, but some of the people . . ." She shook her head and frowned.

"We hate them," said Reuben, looking up from the sack, his brow furrowed. "We especially hate the circus people. Who we especially aren't." He returned to shuffling through our belongings, his mustache fluffier than ever. Kovacsz released the last clasp in the set, and we watched as he slowly pushed open the lid of the trunk with a thin, dislocated arm. He silently rose, limbs-first like a spider, and unfolded himself, popping each joint back in place until he was standing directly behind the inspector.

"I see," the inspector said to us. "You're thinking I have all day to sit here and wait for you to find your identification papers. Perhaps I will use this time to begin filling out a 424." He fluttered his fingers downward.

"Good sir," trilled Marina, "I assure you that we are on the verge of completion! If there has been a delay, it is only because I have been distracted by my admiration for the fine knotting of your kerchief this whole time."

"Oh." The man fondled the knot with the tips of his fingers. "Well, I mean," he said, trying not to smile, "certain standards—it's nothing, really, but—"

"Don't sell yourself short! It's something, it's very much something," said Marina. "It is a simply marvelous knot."

"I too am marveling!" boomed Reuben, sounding like a robot run haywire.

"Well, I have to say, I don't get many compliments," said the inspector as he smoothed the loose ends of the kerchief. "These bumpkins can't tell a French Bow from a Double Bronson. Now, those papers?"

Behind the inspector, Kovacsz was working furiously at the list machine, riffling through the tags, scribbling furiously, pausing occasionally to count our numbers. Once all eight cards were in place, he flashed us a thumbs-up and began doing a soundless victory dance in the back of the shed. Dieter widened his eyes and nodded toward the breadbread trunk. Kovacsz shook his head vehemently, then gestured toward his thighs—the slat rash, I guess.

"Oh, but . . . there is still so much more to compliment! For example"—Marina scanned his face frantically—"your nose. Why, it reminds me of the fine noses of the founding settlers."

"It does?"

"Absolutely!" Marina said, slapping the high counter. Reuben dropped the bag he was shuffling through and kneeled to fake-search even harder. "And those eyes! I love the way they . . . droop."

"Droop?" said the inspector, his eyes drooping even farther. "You think my eyes *droop*?"

"Like honey from a baby spoon!" said Marina.

The inspector frowned, then swiveled his chair and reached toward a folder marked *Infraction Forms:*

403–429. Dieter thrust his chin at Kovacsz and glared, clenching his teeth. Kovacsz sighed and climbed back into the trunk, folding himself effortlessly into his trunk-form and somehow carefully securing each clasp behind him. The metamorphosis was again mesmerizing, but I averted my eyes and tried to appear deeply bored.

"The identification papers!" shouted Reuben, quickly drawing the tattered sheets from the sack. "Here they are, beloved sir. The documentation that will match the names in your files, thereby differentiating us from the non-city-dwellers, those impoverished, unfashionable, poorly groomed people who definitely should not be allowed into the city. Unlike us, in our capacity as city-dwellers. Who should. Be allowed, I mean. Into the city."

Reuben smoothed the papers against his thigh and handed them to the inspector, who received them with a pair of tongs, his nose wrinkling. "I will now review these documents in relation to the registry," he said, shaking lint from the papers, "though it may be difficult, what with my droopy eyes."

The inspector retreated to the back of the shed, holding the papers at arm's length in the tongs. He spread the papers across the examination table with a second set of tongs and pulled a series of levers. Wires and spindles leapt into motion, and a group of name tags came fluttering forward.

We waited in silence, watching the inspector's back as he shuffled through the cards. A second man entered the shack. The inspector glanced up at him and shrugged in our direction, and the man peered at us from beneath an awning of luxurious eyebrow hair. He saw the trunk on the conveyor belt and bent down to inspect the label. Reuben clutched the sack in a white fist. The man poked at the clasp with his forefinger and frowned. He put his thumb on the buckle.

"I hope everything's okay back there?" Marina said, a sliver of fear in her voice. My smile was wilting. The man at the trunk snapped his head toward us. He opened his mouth to say something, but the inspector spoke instead. "Proceed," he said, carrying our papers back to the window with his tongs, looking very much like a droopy-eyed lobster.

"Proceed?" said Marina. "Really?"

The inspector raised an eyebrow. "You seem surprised."

"No, of course, proceed, of course! I'm just excited to return home, is all. Back home to Destina. Where we live. Burford has its distinctive spirit, of course, a certain authenticity, but the residents lack . . . well, I don't want to say *refinement*, and I suppose one can't change one's personal aroma, but—"

"Please, for the love of Madame J, proceed. And take your filthy trunk with you." He turned the conveyor's hand crank until the trunk dropped through the opening on the far side of the shed, eliciting a muffled, Kovacsz-inflected groan of pain.

"Yes, proceed, of course, certainly," Marina said,

throwing her scarf over her shoulder. "Here we go! Thank you so much! Love that kerchief!" The inspector pulled the window shut and locked it.

We squeezed through a narrow gate. Dieter hefted the trunk with Kovacsz inside and we crossed the river, the glass towers of the city ahead glinting with the colors of the setting sun.

DAY FIVE

"OUR LUMINOUS BEACON OF WHATEVER."

by Hank Hamper - The Daily Scrutinizer

The trial muddled onward today, a microcosm of our lonesome pilgrimage toward death. With neither the innocent flush of the beginning nor the bracing finality of the end, we are left with only the long, mechanistic middle, the aimless trudge of our solitary lives. We stumble aimlessly, hoping for a sign—and then, for just an instant, we catch a glimmer. The clouds part, and for that dazzling instant it seems as though there may be another lonely soul out there, someone just like us, or maybe mostly like us but with enough adorable quirks and eccentricities to keep things interesting, and who knows, maybe an exotic pet? And, just perhaps, these two lonely souls could be united in a symphony of spiritual and sexual energy, with or without the pet.

But like all things, those moments of hope die quickly, wilting like metaphorical cobwebs, crumbling like allegorical sand castles, and all that is left behind is the grim stretch of days and our endless labors, while other people have special times alongside other other people, disregarding the exotic pets that they have supposedly been hired specifically to tend.

In totally unrelated news, today's legal proceedings did not include an appearance by Madame J, who was nowhere to be found—at least, not in the courtroom, though there were reports that she was seen at a water-front café, sharing a parfait of mixed berries with . . . oh, forget it. Do I need to describe every gory detail, who was where with whom, who fed whom which variety of berry, who canoodled whom upon what in the shade of which while whatting what? I am a journalist, after all, and thus I will simply present the relevant news-facts: The trial continued. Madame J was not in attendance. Existence is a pungent bucket of crud.

Must we forge onward with this reportage? Apparently we must. And so, as you can probably guess if you've been following this or any other trial ever, it was time for the defense. Kornblatt was wheeled back into the courtroom, his cage now sealed inside a waffled mutedome to neuter any further verbal outbursts, and old Dobler was lowered to the dais as usual, his hands shaking like leaves in a windstorm. As the ancient man with the neck-skin of a flayed turkey struggled to don his vestments, Kornblatt's lawyer shuffled toward the podium, littering stray papers from a seemingly unclaspable briefcase clutched to his chest. Barrister Gentool's recent promotion is further proof of Destina's democratic spirit—from brine-tender to defense attorney, special for this trial.

Gentool sorted through his files, pausing to remove several napkins and a flattened sandwich from the pile. He eventually located the desired document, squinted at it from arm's length, and took a deep breath. "I call to the stand," he said, "the defendant himself . . . Zalty Krumblitt!"

A hush descended over the courtroom—a rustling hush with the force of a din, the sound of a hundred craning necks, a hundred trembling ladies, the scratching of a hundred pencils on a hundred judicial bingos.

Kornblatt slowly climbed the steps to the witness stand, head bowed. He sat, face still shadowed beneath the brim of his battered black hat—and then he looked upward, outward toward the lawyers, past them, at us, the assembled onlookers, his audience. His dark eyes sparkled, and a hint of a smile seemed to play above his sharp chin. I wanted to barf.

At that moment, a member of the Uniformed Youth rushed into the courtroom with a bold swish of orange smock. The sycophantic tot stepped reverently to Dobler's platform and whispered a lengthy message into the judge's drooping cartilaginous sound-hole. The judge arched his brow and narrowed his eyes.

"Attention," said Dobler, furiously banging his gavel, a total cliché of judicial fulmination. "We have received reports of checkpoint permeation. An unkempt mob has been spotted on the city's outskirts, moving inward." Gasps whooshed throughout the courtroom. "Whether the fact that the defendant has apparently summoned a cadre of foot soldiers to storm our capital is a sign of guilt or innocence, I leave for the jury to decide. Double-strength tassel forces have been deployed to prevent any breach of the prison grounds, though I guess I don't know about the rest of the city—actually, they're probably heading this way right now. The defense rests! Today's court proceedings are hereby adjourned."

The judge tugged his hoist-rope and was quickly lifted back through the ceiling. Gentool dropped his note cards, grabbed his briefcase (from which papers flew like the cottony seeds of a dandelion), and sprinted down the aisle and out the courtroom doors, with a swarming crowd of civilians and bailiffs following behind. This reporter remained seated until he was all alone in the cavernous courtroom, staring at that doorway through which our nation's luminous beacon of whatever had passed just twenty-four hours earlier.

I wanted to bang a gavel of my own. "An unkempt mook has been spotted on the Madame's inskirts," I'd announce. "Apparently all she wanted was a beardo with a spray bottle. This century's life proceedings are hereby adjourned. Everyone go home and sit in your J shrine and weep yourself drunk."

In any case, the trial is now officially over, and

Kornblatt has been sent back to his cell atop the Needle. There he sits, high above the Termination Field, he and the field both awaiting the jury's decision. Will we utilize our newly refurbished execution facilities (now featuring a croc pool and the Holy Roller), or was that just a big waste of time and money? How does it feel, I wonder, to be suspended in the balance like that? Having one's fate rest entirely in someone else's hands, whether they be a hangman's hairy meathooks or delicate white ladyfingers?

There is only one way to find out: I must enter the mind of the madman. I must journey to the Confinement Needle. I must let the darkness consume me.

SOURCE CITIZEN

[Flora Bialy]

RANK

[0239]

RECIPE NAME

[Salty-Sour Egg Kissers]

INGREDIENTS

[Poultry ovum; poultry lips; poultry salt]

INSTRUCTIONS

We crossed the bridge and camped under a hairbush on the far side, hardly even noticing the steady rain of rashy bristles. At daybreak we continued along the road, which gradually gave way to gentle green slopes that rolled down to the bustling city ahead. Reuben's mustache whipped and fluttered in the warm breeze, and Martin Van Buren kept pace at Valentino's side, barely wheezing at all. The air tasted like nectar. We passed through a neighborhood of clean metal warehouses and orderly supply lots, and then a cantilevered market shaded by a billowing blue sail. Tides of shoppers surged through the aisles of the market, filling their carts with fresh produce and baked things we couldn't identify. There were no dusty jars, no briny funk. Gliders passed overhead, soaring up toward the large commercial air barges that crowded the perimeter of the city. We could smell the fragrance of fresh tedfruit from the road and it made us dizzy with hunger, but we kept moving.

The streets of Destina were slick and glassy to accommodate the silk trucks. Everyone around us clutched fancy new scrollers and wore pixelcloud vests, and the sound was deafening. I had never been in the city before. None of us had, except for Kovacsz, years ago, before the flood. It was brighter now, he said. Cleaner. Everything seemed designed to cast or reflect light. I squinted through the glare, looking for something that resembled a prison. I thought maybe it was underground, because all I could see were sidewalk cafés, touchless pet groomers, smoothie bars. Was this city's prison housed inside a smoothie bar? It seemed possible somehow.

"Excuse me, ma'am," Dieter said to a woman wheeling a triple-wide baby carriage. "Could you point us toward the jail, please?" The woman glanced at him, unfurled a mirrored curtain around the carriage, and hurried down the sidewalk.

"You haven't the face for streetwork, Dieter," said Reuben, stepping in front of him to approach a florist in a yellowscotch suit wrapping bundles in his stall. "My dear sir," he said, "I couldn't pass by your establishment without remarking on your keen outfit." The man looked up from his shearwork. "By way of background, a dear friend of ours is currently being held in the local correctional facility. All a misunderstanding, of course! Quite comical, actually. Funnier still is our own lack of understanding regarding the whereabouts of said facility. Imagine our predicament! So, my question being, might you possess enlightenment upon that topic? The whereabouts, I mean?"

The flower man squinted at Reuben, who, I now realized, was draped in the same canvas poncho he had been wearing since Burford. "If you're referring to the prison needle," he said, "it's for prisoners. A prisoner is your friend? I believe the word for that is *accomplice*."

Reuben raised a finger. "My good man, I must quibble with you on that one. Friendship is a winged bird that knows no walls, a bond that transcends any label or barrier, despite the—"

An elderly shopper with a handful of azaleas leaned toward the florist. "That talk sounds like terrorist talk to me," she said in a low voice. "Not that I'd know what terrorist talk sounds like. But that's what it sounds like."

I grabbed Reuben by his poncho and dragged him away from the stall. We all huddled under an awning, trying not to look as lost as we felt. I searched the crowds, hunting for a friendly face. Marina squinted past my shoulder, craned her neck, and then pointed to the east. There, beyond the cobbled streets, above the canal-striped parkland, rose a thin black spire. The prison needle.

We kept our eyes on the tower as we followed it across the city, through the twisting alleyways of the fashion district, the sprawling gardens, the river-wide thorough-fares, always with that dark needle rising above, growing taller and broader as the afternoon faded into dusk. We wound our way through the ethnic quarter, thickly for-ested with skewers and smoke, and finally emerged onto a promenade, a white gravel path that led to a tall stone wall that encircled the tower itself. Inside that tower, some-where, was Zloty.

We approached the wall, which was sharply reflective, its surface reinforced by a self-lubricating glaze, though its height alone seemed sufficient to repel any aspiring intruders. If it was this hard to get in, I could only imagine what'd be involved in getting out. We looked at our dim reflections in the gleaming black stone, slowly realizing the obvious: the people who built a wall like this wouldn't be interested in hearing about a funny misunderstand-ing. No one was going to open the door and let Zloty stroll out. If we wanted him, we'd have to go get him. Somehow.

The good news was, we were alone; the area was com-pletely deserted, the only sign of humanity a few stray drifts of trash caught in the scrubby grass. The bad news was that we were alone on the wrong side of the wall.

"What we need," said Kovacsz, "is to somehow pen-etrate this wall."

"If only someone could apply a great deal of force," Sharon said. "Thereby producing a hole to allow our pas-sage through. If only!"

They chuckled, and even I allowed myself a smile: for once, a challenge we were actually ready to meet. We needed to smash a wall, and our group just happened to include a remarkably effective mobile wall-smashing unit.

We all stepped aside, looking at Dieter expectantly. He looked back, expressionless.

"Um, Dieter?" said Sharon, tilting her head toward the wall.

"Yes?" he said, monotone, heavy-lidded.

"The wall?" she said. "Could you, like, make it go away?"

He craned his neck, scanning the black expanse as it faded into the darkening sky. "Make it go away? How do you propose I do that?"

"That thing you do. You know, smash. Demolish, disintegrate, whatever."

"Is that what I am to you?" Dieter said, flicking his hand in the air. "A brainless basher of objects? Some kind of mobile wall-smashing unit? Just point me at the nearest wall and push my Smash button, is that it?"

I poked at a pebble in the dirt and tried not to meet his eyes. Reuben finally broke the silence.

"Dieter, it's not like that. You know it's not like that. Or, maybe it happens to be just a tad like that at the moment, but we know you're a very talented individual—an artist, I mean. And I enjoy a good miming as much as the next guy. Enjoy and *respect*," he said emphatically, starting to believe it himself. "But at the moment, just in terms

of strict effectiveness and problem solving and whatnot . . . well, I'm just thinking that in this one particular
case, miming—while certainly the higher art form, don't
get me wrong—might not be the right medium for this particular moment in time, whereas smashing, that prehis-
toric aesthetic vocation, is possibly more useful here?"

Dieter folded his arms and frowned.

"This isn't a show, Dieter," said Sharon. "This is for
real. This is for Zloty."

Dieter looked at her, sighed, and took a few steps toward the wall. He ran his finger along the surface and
sniffed it, then reared back, clenched a fist, and drove it
into the wall. Cracks spiderwebbed from the impact, but
the wall stood. He reared back again and this time came
forward almost gently, striking the wall in the same spot.
The stone fell away in a cloud of black powder, and we
found ourselves peering through to the other side.

Beyond the wall was a tract of brittle yellow grass,
leading to the needle itself, a flat black spear that seemed
to cut the sky in half. Its surface was, like the outer wall,
smooth as glass, marked only with a scattering of narrow
windows and calcified stains. The sky had purpled with
twilight, but the tower seemed to cast a deeper darkness
of its own.

Dieter stood in front of the hole, arms loose, fists
still clenched. He let out another long sigh and stepped
aside to let us through—but then he froze. His eyes

went wide, and then we heard it, too: voices, two of them, on the other side of the wall. The voices became louder as they steadily approached, saying things like "I really think I heard something" and then "I know what a *bird* sounds like" and then "What's that pile of rubble doing there next to that wall?" and finally "Hey, wait a second . . ."

We stood, paralyzed by fear, gaping at the ragged hole. Through the settling dust two guards came into view on the other side. Even amid the terror, my first thought was: Those are some stupid-looking hats. And they were—both men wore floppy blue caps with a pointy brass medallion drooping off either side and a silk tassel dangling from each droop. The men, heavily mustachioed, stared at us from behind the tassels. They peered through the hole, frowning, eyes darting from side to side, tassels swaying.

"This," began the first guard, bushy mustache fluttering quizzically, "this does not seem right."

The other man, whose mustache was long and slick, with scythe-like handles, replied, "It certainly does not seem not wrong. That much is for certain."

"How long have we been patrolling this wall?" the first one said. "Years. Multiple years. And in all that time, have we ever seen a portion of the wall that resembles this? I can't say that I have."

The guard with the thin mustache blinked just as a

pebbled chunk of mortar fell to the ground a few feet from where he stood. "I can't say that I have, either. This particular section of the wall appears to be . . . well, it appears to not entirely be. Rather, it would be more accurate to say that part of this wall appears to be elsewhere."

None of us had moved, or even breathed, this entire time. We were just out of sight, pressed up against the other side of the wall, the guards only inches away. I could've reached out and stroked that bushier mustache, which was now twitching furiously, like a hungry bunny. Any closer and we'd surely be discovered.

"Well," said the other, "this'll be a what? A 292.g, Portion of Wall Misplaced, Whereabouts Unknown?"

The guard pressed his hand against his lip to stop the twitching. "That seems a bit premature. Can we really be so sure that the whereabouts are unknown? Probably safer to start with a Category 9-K filing."

"You think we need to bring in the locational epistemologist? On a Friday?"

"Afraid so, my good friend. And also the shatterbolt squad, just in case anything's on the other side. You heard the orders this morning. High alert, cruddy interlopers, all that."

"They always make such a mess. Just because we're outdoors doesn't mean you can leave bloody corpses lying around willy-nilly." He sighed. "But I suppose you're right. Shall we blow our whistle?" he said, fishing deep into his coat pocket.

My heart sank. We were trapped—snared before we even began to sneak.

I heard a rustle and turned to see Dieter breathing hard, turning inward, readying himself. He closed his eyes for a moment and clenched his jaw. I saw him give the tiniest of nods before opening his eyes again, wide and severe. He leapt forward.

I cringed, covering my face. I'd seen what Dieter could do to a solid stone wall or a bushel of tedfruit— I didn't want to imagine what he'd unleash upon a couple prison guards armed only with slumber clubs and nasal spray. I knew these were desperate times, but still I had no desire to personally witness the brutal takedown, the floppy-hatted dismemberment, the once-bushy mustaches now drenched with blood. I crouched behind the wall, bracing myself for the howls of agony.

But I heard nothing. Not just nothing, but somehow less than that—an active void of sound. I turned back toward the hole.

Dieter was hunched forward, balanced on the balls of his feet, his chin jutting out from his chest. He had his hands up, palms out, fingers splayed. He patted the air in front of the hole, swiping at it, running his hands back and forth and up and down along an invisible plane, mere inches from the guards' faces. They stared, transfixed. No one spoke. Dieter continued to slide his hands through the air, reaching forward again and again, each time stopping in the space where the wall once stood.

The two guards stood frozen in contemplation. The bushier one opened his mouth and then closed it. The other opened his own mouth and left it that way.

"Upon further examination," said the first, "I might want to revise my initial opinion."

"I was just thinking the same thing," said the other. "I can't say it looks exactly the same as other walls I've seen. But there's clearly a wall there—I feel sure of that."

His partner squinted. "I feel the same way. I wasn't sure how to say it, but you—you've described it perfectly."

"Not all walls are the same."

"Certainly not."

"Brick walls, stone walls. Ham."

"Ham?"

"In Dunsk they have a wall of ham, I've heard. Does it repel the vegetarian insurgents? Who knows? But that's my point! Who are we to discriminate, to pick and choose which wall counts as a wall? That's not our job. Our job is to finish walking this circle, and then do it again, and keep going till someone tells us to stop."

"Also to fill out forms, when appropriate."

"Of course. Without a doubt. But you and I have seen that there is a wall here. Beyond seeing—we've *experienced* the wall, am I right? Is there a form for 'Wall Here, Somehow Different, but Still Definitely Here'? I think not. So let's continue on our rounds, shall we?"

The guards paused, tilted their heads, and gave another

glance at Dieter's flattened palm. And then, with a flash of tassel, they were gone.

I looked at Dieter in disbelief, but he appeared entirely unsurprised. He counted to ten in whispers, then disappeared through the hole. We followed.

DAY SIX

"MINOR LEAKAGE."

by Hank Hamper - The Daily Scrutinizer

I awoke early, in a pool of my own sorrow, pondering the jury's ongoing deliberations. Would Kornblatt be found guilty and sentenced to a painful, flamboyant death? Or would he receive the far crueler punishment: continued existence upon this gray earth, eaten alive from the inside out, not by ratfish or wolf crabs but by one's own hopes and dreams.

For him, probably the first; for me, apparently the second. But is there really so much difference between criminal madness and unrequited love? Is Kornblatt merely farther down a path that awaits us all? What is it like to stare this finality direct in the face? Is there remorse? Terror? Perhaps even a strange grace? I needed to visit Kornblatt himself. I needed to see just how low a man could sink. I envied his imminent oblivion.

I presented my identification at the door to the

Confinement Needle, under the watchful eyes and pointed shatterbolts of six hulking guards. Their hunger for destruction was palpable, aromatic. I hoped they would smash my face in. They didn't.

The door swung open, revealing the infamous barb-beam security corridor, capable of incinerating a fly mid-buzz. I considered sprinting down the hall, the lasers or whatever zapping me into sweet numb dust. Instead, I waited like a dumb cow. A guard at the far end deactivated the beams with a large red switch, and I walked down a metal path into the core of the tower.

I was escorted to the top floor of the Needle by an enthusiastic prison concierge, who peppered me with fun facts along the way. Did I know the facility had suffered not a single escape in its entire proud history? Did I care to purchase authorized souvenirs at the gift shop? No, I didn't know. No, I didn't care. As we climbed the stairs, I felt a strange chill emanating from the smooth stone walls, and commented on the unexpected draft. That's no draft, I was told—that's our shadowy prongmaster, a nameless assassin trained from birth to do nothing but aim, throw, and kill. He lives in the heating ducts of the prison. Oh, I said, and felt another icy breeze from behind. I bared my throat to a vent, but there was only silence and wretched interminable survival.

Finally we arrived at Kornblatt's cell, a musty gray cube thick with misery and resignation. Perfect. I demanded to go inside. The guards frowned, protested, and pleaded, but I was resolute, proclaiming the importance of a well-informed press. They opened the heavy door and I stepped in. The lock clicked shut behind me.

And there we were, alone together. I stared at Kornblatt. He stared at me. We were like two travelers at the end of the world. Two ancient gladiators, eternal enemies united by a shared, hard-won wisdom. No one spoke. No one moved.

"Hello there!" he said. "Welcome to my quarters. I'm afraid I can't offer any refreshments—the amenities here are quite limited. Nevertheless, allow me to introduce myself: the name is Zloty, and the game is . . . Sir, are you *crying*? What's wrong?"

Apparently there was some minor leakage emerging from my eye region. I wiped them dry and began to explain—and then collapsed into tears, great heaving sobs. Kornblatt rushed forward, leg shackles clinking, and embraced me; I buried my face in his vinegary prison garb and wept and wept.

I of course oppose everything this heinous man does, thinks, and signifies. I can hardly wait to see him battered and deep-fried. But there is a fundamental power to the communion of shared pain, even if one sharer is sleeping in his self-made deathbed and the other is a blameless soldier of love. Even a creature like Kornblatt, hurtling inevitably toward gruesome dismemberment, can see that some men deserve a better fate.

"Well," I sniffled, "there's a woman involved."

"And she is in grave danger? Afflicted with swampfoot? Kidnapped by barge hounds?"

"No, no, none of that. She's fine. She just doesn't know I exist."

"Ah, yes." He smiled. "Fortunately, that is the easiest problem to remedy!"

"It is?"

"Of course it is! Do you not exist?"

"I do."

"So there you go! If you didn't exist, this would be much more difficult—though not impossible, I once met a man who was happily married to an imaginary goat, but the logistics are difficult, I can't deny. I mean, their children—"

"But there's someone else," I said. "They've been . . . sharing parfait."

"Obstacles!" He waved his hand. "Let me tell you a story. When I was seventeen years old, I was drafted into the Gurdash Preemption. Before I knew it, I was packed into a train car with forty-three confused, itchy Spaghetts, rumbling through the darkness. We had no possessions except the standard-issue supply sack: kneepads, goggles, and a soup sponge. The boy next to me soiled himself in fear before the engine even started. Another soldier, a bigboned fellow, tried to climb out the window but got stuck halfway and had to ride like that, dangling, until the checkpoint three hours later. It was not a happy night."

Kornblatt paused to adjust his hat.

"When the train finally stopped, we were ordered to grab our sacks and start marching—all the way from Clurt to the border, twenty-one days of walking through burned-out nothingness, headed to probable death. The fear was bad, but the boredom was worse. Eventually, though, the marching became a sort of music, and by day seventeen I had composed an entire mobile symphony, a costumed fantasia of boots, mud, and agonized groans. I taught the opening motif to my shacklemate, and he began clomping in tune. Another conscript fashioned delightful masks from his own pants, stitched together with his own hair, and I carved an old yam into a serviceable bassoon. Soon the full squadron was stepping, squishing, and moaning in unison. It was glorious. For those moments, we almost forgot our troubles, our dangers, our surroundings.

"Which might have been part of the reason why, just before the climactic overture, we fell into a pit of suckmud. By the time I was belched out, a hundred yards down the hill, I was alone, with no sign of my fellow marchers. I don't know if they perished in the mud or continued on to the front. I wandered to the nearest village, dripping and filthy, the now-empty shackle dangling from my leg. I asked for a blacksmith, someone who could free me from the chain. Instead I was brought to Dieter, who at the time was employed as the town's moving van. He snapped it off with one hand. I was agog, and signed him to an exclusive contract right then and there. The rest, of course, is history, a trail of happy crowds from here to Tubuntsi. My point is, you just need to work, and wait, and believe. Flowers, songs, whatever it takes. You seem like a sensible, sensitive fellow—I'm sure she'll come around."

"You are? She will?"

"Without a doubt. If I hadn't been drafted, put on that train, fallen into the mud—if not for all that, I may have never founded the Carnument! Who knows where I'd be today?" Kornblatt paused for a moment, glancing around the cell, then quickly shook his head. "There are always obstacles," he continued, "but obstacles merely show us the path. They are just rungs on the ladder, trampolines to triumph. It's like the old saying, 'A pickle is just a cucumber plus—'"

Rungs on ladder, I scribbled in my notebook. *Trampolines to triumph. Pants masks.* The criminal underbelly does have a certain salty wisdom, that can't be denied. *Obstacles are there to be stepped upon.*

I got to my feet and then I— Reader, I don't know where I found the courage, the grace, but I *embraced* the man. I hurried out of the cell, the door locked tight behind me, and proceeded to exit the vile, stinking prison. Before me was the gleaming Termination Field, the full array of devices and potential conclusions. Kornblatt will reach his end seventy-two hours from now, but for the rest of us, new beginnings are still possible. There are ladders to be climbed, obstacles to be trampled. Yes, sometimes we are lost, alone, deep in a pit of suck-mud—but that is not the end. To find the light on the other side, we must first tunnel through the muck. We must be willing to get our fingers a little dirty.

RECIPE NAME

[Scouse Wallies]

INGREDIENTS

[Buy direct from factory]

INSTRUCTIONS

We stepped through the hole in the wall and entered the vast prison yard. Night had fallen and the world was a mesh of shadows. We could just barely make out the shape of the needle against the purple sky. A muffled loudspeaker squawked random letters and numbers, and guards at the front gate waved their flashlights aimlessly over the grounds. We needed a place to hide, to plan, so we crept in a huddled group toward a mass of dark structures, weird jutting spires and minarets—some sort of strange sculpture garden, it seemed. We groped the rough surfaces until Bruce found a cavity big enough for all of us to hide in. "Flora, you stand watch," Kovacsz said, and then immediately fell into a dead sleep on the dusty brick floor. The others took their cue from him and within a minute I was the only one awake.

Zloty was close—trapped high above, with many guards and obstacles between us and him, but still: close. Terrifying failure surely awaited us tomorrow, but we had already made it farther than I'd ever expected. Leaning into a sliver of weak moonlight, I scribbled another letter to no one and fed it into the scroller. I imagined the words bouncing among the gherkins and krauts and half-sours, finally arriving at some bewildered reader in Klobouk or Ploly or Spagg, and then the merciful crumpling, the immediate forgetting, the eternal obsolescence.

When I opened my eyes, dawn was just taking hold. The yard was quiet, but a wash of grainy sunlight fell through the small opening of our shelter. I crawled over to the entrance and cautiously peered outside. We were in the middle of what appeared to be a sort of carnival grounds— a stage with an arched lighting scaffold, flanked by vast banks of bleachers, and, all around us, an assemblage of brightly colored thrill rides. But not the fun kind. These rides were more like the kind you'd visit only once. Because afterward you'd be dead, I mean. I saw elegant hanging poles, a frothing toxin bath, and three different varieties of guillotine, as well as less familiar structures: a giant iron fist clutching a dozen oscillating swords, some kind of free-fall tower with a splintery diving board at the top, a tank swarming with small albino crocodiles, and a gargantuan animatronic priest with sparking coils for fingers. I looked above the doorway of our brick hut and saw IMMOLATION CABANA! painted in cheerful, flame-licked script.

One by one, I nudged the others awake and indicated our predicament.

"Of course it is thus," said Kovacsz. "Nothing is ever as it seems; rather, things are always worse, or, as in this case, much worse."

Marina cleared ashes from a wall vent, which gave us a view of the door that led into the prison itself, surrounded by six guards armed with shatterbolts. These were not the gullible, tassel-clad guards we'd encountered at the wall. They were bigger, broader, with sharp, overhung features and teardrop-shaped helmets that glinted in the gathering sunlight.

"They probably haven't filled in Dieter's hole yet," said Bruce. "If we make a run for it, I bet we could still get out of here."

"And there's no checkpoint on the bridge *leaving* Destina," Marina said. "We'll be safe in Burford by nightfall."

There was a long pause. In the distance we heard metallic clattering, fuzzy loudspeakers, shuffling feet. I thought back to Burford, our tilted tents, what we had left behind, what was no longer there, what still needed to be done.

"Remember the time in Grütn?" I said quietly. They all turned. "When the underground fermenter ruptured and the whole town turned into a vinegar swamp and our big top dissolved? We thought that was the end. But then

Zloty sewed a new tent from old tuber sacks, and we put on a show that night."

"The new tent also dissolved, that same night," said Dieter.

"Our boots did, too. My entire foot-skin peeled off, in one piece, just like a snake," said Kovacsz. "I haven't worn sandals in public ever since."

"Flora's right, though," Reuben said. "These guards do pose something of a challenge, no doubt. But it's like Zloty always said: 'A pickle is just a cucumber plus time.'"

"Also salt," said Sharon.

"Or vinegar," added Bruce.

"Personally, I like to throw in a pinch of turmeric," said Valentino, stepping forward. "But enough dithering. I know what you are all thinking, and the answer is yes: Martin Van Buren would be happy to eliminate these men. It is, after all, his natural jungle instinct."

"Eliminate?" said Kovacsz. "Jungle?" The dog was curled up in the corner gnawing a long, knobby shinbone, which I chose to believe was from a very large chicken. With very large shins.

"Valentino, this is serious," said Dieter, punching his own thigh to emphasize the seriousness.

Valentino frowned. "Believe me, I would not suggest deploying Martin Van Buren if this wasn't serious. You doubt the sufficient ferocity of this beast? You doubt his razor-sharp pincers, his lust for blood? We will show you."

"Don't show us, for Jesu."

Valentino took Martin Van Buren's head in his hands and rested his forehead against the bridge of the dog's long snout. He whispered something into Martin's ears, first one and then the other, and then kissed the dog on its head and patted its flank. It stood and shook itself awake with a pathetic rattle.

"I cannot watch this," said Kovacsz, turning away. "Dogs are simply large vermin, but even vermin deserve a sporting chance. This is certain obliteration."

Valentino led the dog to the doorway, where it hesitated for a moment, looking mournfully back at the bone.

Sharon grabbed Valentino by the shoulder. "I swear, if you get us killed—"

"You'll what?" Bruce snapped. "We'll all be crubbing dead."

"Which is sort of my point, you literalist cretin."

Valentino raised his hand for silence. The dog stood at the entrance for a long minute, just sniffing. He gingerly put one paw down on the gravel, and then another. Eventually he disappeared. We listened from inside the brick hut as he crunched his way along the gravel path. We could hear the guards speaking quietly to one another, and then they started to laugh when they caught sight of Martin. One of them whistled and clapped for the dog to come closer, and the laughter grew louder. Kovacsz glared at Valentino, who was standing tall, alert and entirely unconcerned, as if he were waiting in the wings before a Tuesday matinee.

And then we heard a low, ragged growling, more machine than animal. The men abruptly stopped laughing. The growl spiked and flared, and we heard grunting, boots scuffing against gravel. The growl escalated into a jagged whine followed by a series of harsh, percussive barks. Some of the men sprinted past the Immolation Chamber, kicking up gravel against the walls of our hut, and I heard snatches of speech: "Grabth—" and "Donlet—" and "Hel—" The barking was relentless, louder and louder until it was the only thing I could hear. And then it stopped.

Valentino peered out the doorway. "Yes, looks like we're clear now," he said, emerging briskly into the yard, where Martin Van Buren sat, struggling to bite an insect off his hindquarters. Valentino dug in his pocket for a scrap of jerky and threw it to Martin, who sneezed with gratitude. There was no sign of the guards, just some overturned helmets, scattered tassel fronds, and a single boot resting in the gravel. Directly ahead of us was a simple wooden door in the side of the prison tower.

"What was our plan again?" Reuben said, looking up at the point where the needle disappeared into the clouds.

"Get Zloty," Marina said.

"That was actually, well, a bit of a rhetorical question, meant in part to showcase how little of a plan we actually have, seeing as how we do not know where in this formidable structure Zloty actually is, although certainly there isn't much to do in any case but go straight up."

"And guess what we're going to do?"

Reuben nodded, and went to try the handle, not expecting it to turn. It did. He looked back at us. We all shrugged, so he pulled the door open, tentatively and then all at once. Inside was a bare corridor lined with perforated metal walls, illuminated only by the sunlight spilling through the doorway. There was no sign of other guards, no shrieking alarms. Reuben looked back at us again. We shrugged again.

"Hold on," he said. "My cousin who no longer has legs told me never to trust a strange metal hallway." He picked up a pebble and threw it down the hall. A bright line shot out of the wall, turning the pebble into a purplish plume of pebble dust.

Bruce sniffed the corridor, which suddenly smelled like the air before a thunderstorm.

"Seems to be protected by a beam of some sort," he said.

"A beam of some sort?" Sharon said. "Wow. Such precise terminology."

"I'll terminologize *you*."

She snorted. "Even if that was an actual thing a person could do, I'm pretty sure you'd suck at it."

"Oh, piss in your own mouth," Bruce said.

Sharon bent down and scooped up two of the guards' gleaming steel helmets. Bruce flinched and stepped backward. "Come on, don't be such a baby," she said. "Remember the show in Truddle?"

"Mating Beetles, you mean?" said Bruce. "Slightly different circumstances, obviously, but . . . yes, I suppose it could work."

"You want floor or walls?"

"I'd better stick with walls—you were always the master of this one."

Sharon tossed the helmets to Bruce and picked up a third, which she also threw his way, just as the first helmet was coming back to her. As they continued the smooth exchange, Sharon backed up to the doorway and lowered herself until she was lying on the ground, still juggling the helmets with Bruce.

I held my breath as she slowly inched her way into the target zone. The first beam fired with a brilliant flash and bounced harmlessly off the helmet's steel surface back to the wall, where it sizzled and sparked. The next beam met the same fate. Sharon continued pushing herself down the corridor with her feet, catching and tossing back the helmets to Bruce, who followed behind in a careful rhythm. It looked like love.

Within a minute they were down the corridor, where Bruce flipped a large red switch to disable the projectors. We hissed a near-silent cheer of victory and charged down the hall. Bruce extended his hand to Sharon, who took it gracefully. He pulled her up and she smiled demurely at him.

"Just like old times, huh?" she said. "Me on my back and you hardly even trying."

"Allow me to reiterate: piss in your own mouth."

I hustled them along the hallway, which wound to the right and then the left, dead-ending at a dark stairwell. We climbed the stairs single-file, our shoulders grazing the walls of the narrow passage that, we hoped, would bring us to the apex of the needle where, we hoped, Zloty was imprisoned. We scaled flight after flight until finally reaching the top, which opened onto a slender corridor lit by water lamps. I was next to last, with only Marina behind me, so I could barely make out a steel door at the far end of the corridor. But it smelled right—the distinctive scent of old vinegar and mustache oil. Zloty was near.

I had just begun sprinting down the hallway when I heard a quick swish from behind, more like the shadow of a noise than an actual sound. I turned and saw a man in matte black armor drop through a hatch in the ceiling, landing in a fighting stance between Marina and me. He drew two prongs from a quiver strapped to his thigh and pointed the pointy ends at Marina.

We all froze in terror—all except Marina, who turned to face the black-suited man. He reared back and hurled the needles at her with a dispassionate precision, looking almost bored to have such an easy target. I clamped my eyes shut to avoid the sight of Marina's evisceration, but no howls of agony followed. I cracked open a single eyelid to see Marina still standing against the far wall, now smiling provocatively. The prongs were buried in the wall, quivering from the impact, one on either side of her face. Puzzled, the man drew another set of prongs from his thigh-holster and flung them at Marina. Again they plunged into the wall, this time just outside her ribs. The assassin reached for a third set and a fourth, his agitation and dismay becoming apparent with each failed attack. Marina never flinched, never spoke, just stood there with that maddeningly casual smile.

Now all out of prongs, the assassin plucked a set of shurikens from his shoulder armor. He winged all six of them at once, and they sunk into the wall in a silver halo above Marina's head. He pulled a blowgun from an arm sheath and fired a fusillade of poison darts, which articulated a feather-tipped outline of Marina's body on the wall. Panicked, he ran his hands throughout his armor for something else to throw, but all his holsters, quivers, and pockets were empty. He fell to his knees, his cloth mask darkening with tears.

Marina sauntered up to the weeping man and rested her hand on his sweaty head. "Great working with you," she whispered. "Call me sometime!" She stepped over his fetal heap and sprinted down the hall to where I stood, gaping.

A loudspeaker in the wall sputtered to life. "All units, foreign elements are advancing through the corridors. Proceed to alert level tan. Operate with speed notch periwinkle. Use force degree umber."

I didn't like the sound of that umber. This wasn't getting any easier.

"In here!" Reuben said, yanking on a small hatch that led into a dim, musty room. It wasn't Zloty's cell, but it also wasn't a corridor, which made it just right for our immediate needs. We crawled in and closed the hatch behind us.

DAY SEVEN

"I MUST ACCEPT SOME BLAME."

by Hank Hamper - The Daily Scrutinizer

Breaking news: a rogue agent attempting to infiltrate the most intimate regions of our nation has been exposed, apprehended, and eradicated.

I am, of course, referring to Madame J's cloudy-eyed "assistant," the uppity spray-toter. This misting mister is a threat no longer, his campaign of distraction undone by, ironically, his own distraction. Yes: amid his filthy swirl of woo, he neglected his fundamental duty, the perpetual moistening of dear Simeon.

We're still piecing together the details, but it appears that the perpetrator left the central residence at approximately 11:00 a.m., saying he was "popping out" in order to "score [a bottle of] OJ and extra saline [solution]." His subsequent whereabouts are currently unknown, but he remained absent from the residence for the remainder of the day. When Madame J returned to her sleeping quarters (O holy sanctum) that evening, she found poor Simeon desiccating on a throw rug, parched and crusty. She of course hates to see any living thing in discomfort, but Simeon . . . I can't even imagine. The hairy-faced underling was immediately summoned, whereupon he spun an outlandish story of improbable traffic jams, enigmatic misinformation, a masked man obstructing him at every turn. Really, a masked man? Some sort of heroic nemesis? Who would possibly want to do something like that, dear reader?

The employee has been transferred to Outer Spagg, where he will spend the rest of his days stirring a brine tub in some drab hamlet.

Readers, I know what you're thinking. You've been trying to clue me in on this all along. You were wary of this hirsute gentleman right from the start. I'm kicking myself because I was blind to it. Never saw an issue with the guy. Sure, I may have noticed that, over time, he seemed to be less interested in performing the job he was hired for and more interested in following the Madame around like an orphaned ferret. But I let my personal troubles interfere with my journalistic responsibilities, and for that I can only beg your forgiveness. I just never suspected a thing, even when the authorities came by my house last night to tell me the news, interrupting my lengthy session in the exfoliating drum, proving conclusively that I couldn't possibly have had anything to do with the incident, not that I needed an alibi, but still. I guess ol' Hank failed you, readers. You saw all this coming. I'm ashamed at myself but proud of you. And very, very glad that this "Mister" character is now neck-deep in dill broth.

Simeon, briefly thought to be beyond rescue, is now recovering in a temperature-controlled nutrient bath. Madame J is recovering as well—shaken by the incident, of course, but also strengthened, liberated, newly luminous. God, such a light emanates from that woman. I can hardly stand it. I mean, I *would* stand it, if offered the chance. I'd stand right in front of it, naked and unafraid, ready to place my very soul in Madame's small white hands.

And it is those hands and that luminous glow that our nation needs now more than ever—for even as we apprehended the malefactor penetrating from within, his unwashed counterparts have been penetrating from without. Yes: the invaders have successfully slithered into the Confinement Needle, the innermost boudoir of our nation. The onslaught included rabid beasts slobbering wantonly, married people doing sick married things, and a masochistic harridan clad in tight clothes. Our tree of fear has finally borne fruit, and these are some bad apples indeed.

Fortunately, we now have them right where we want them. Each step these loathsome predators take is actually a step deeper into our trap, a step closer to the center of our web. All guards have been supplied with photographs of the malefactors, so now all we need to do is wait for their inevitable arrival. They can flutter and dart, like frightened bugs, but that will only sticken the stickiness. And when they have fully entangled themselves in our strands, the spider shall approach, pincers gnashing and wet with waiting. (Spider = justice, in case you got lost in the metaphor.)

Sooner rather than later, I hope. Madame J has been through so much lately. The thought of her experiencing a moment of concern over these vile infiltrators—her furrowed brow, her pursed lips, her small hands clenched into worried fists as she sits on the edge of a white-sheeted bed . . .

Citizens, the time for pussyfooting is over. The time for dillying, for dallying. No more can we use rhetoric as a replacement for deeds. No more can I hide behind words, yearning instead of learning, using sentiment to substitute for—see, I'm doing it again. No, this is a new era, a new me. The misting mister was a slithering turd of mankind, of course, but nevertheless I owe him a debt of gratitude, for he has awoken me, and not a moment too soon. Love is a fragile thing, an exotic flower that withers without vigilant care. If we are lucky enough in our eye-blink lives to encounter even a *chance* at this rare blessing, we must treat it as the sacred imperative that it is. We must raise our voice, make ourselves known. I have wasted too much time already. Love is sweet and life is short.

Oh, speaking of: in other news, I've neglected to mention that we decided to kill Kornblatt. I mean, the jury decided. Also, "execute," not "kill." But yeah, it's really happening, day after tomorrow, to allow him sufficient time for fearful anticipation. To facilitate this traditional preexecution Solitary Contemplation of Failure, Kornblatt's cell will be watched by only a single guard, just to make sure he doesn't off himself and ruin everything. And then, come Tuesday, we'll zap the stuffing out of him or tourniquet his face or feed him to the pitchfork eels or who knows—details and methodology are still TBD, but I sure am looking forward to it.

RECIPE NAME

[Solid-Lump Bachelor Relish]

INGREDIENTS

[Solid lumps of bachelor relish]

INSTRUCTIONS

The hatch led to some sort of employee lounge. There were bunk-style hammocks hanging from the ceiling, a small kitchen area with biscuit humidors and a cheese pot, a laundry bin full of crumpled uniforms, and a tassel repair station. Luckily, the room was empty—apparently because everyone in the prison was out looking for us. Muffled announcements streamed through the corridors outside and we heard footsteps clomping below us.

"Until they find us, no one will be lounging in this lounge," Dieter said. "But if we leave, they'll catch us immediately, and the lounging will recommence. It's almost a metaphor for the human condition."

"After centuries of examination and pondering," said

Kovacsz, "the human condition turns out to be a foot-stinking locker room in a dank prison tower. I wish someone had warned me years ago."

"Bruce's face is kind of a metaphor for the human condition," mused Sharon. "Nasty, brutish, and full of crusty boogers."

"Well, Sharon's face is a metaphor for, like, her butt," said Bruce. "They both spew hot foul air from between flabby—"

"Please, friends, let us focus," said Reuben. "Fleets of guards seek to intercept us before we can intercept Zloty."

"With so many guards running around," said Marina, pawing through the laundry bin, "who would notice a few more?" She pulled out a wrinkled orange jumpsuit.

It was a nonsensically simple idea, but nonsense had gotten us this far. We dove into the bin, searching for garments approximating our own sizes.

"All hail the tasselmaster," Valentino shouted, tipping an officer's cap theatrically. Martin Van Buren barked twice, confused, and then curled up on the floor, looking like an old man in a bathhouse. Dieter slipped a foot into a pair of stiff fatigues and they split in two. Somehow I ended up with three elbow pads and a purple sash.

Over the sound of zipping zippers and swaying tassels, I heard a familiar grinding noise. There, sitting on a table by the entrance, was a large institutional-grade scroller slowly spitting out a page. At the top it read

Infiltrator Alert: Wanted Alive or At Least Not Entirely Dead.
Next came our names and ID numbers, one smudgy line
at a time. Everyone huddled around the table to watch.
The machine paused, and I thought the document was
complete—but then the grinding began again, and the
curling paper began to reveal photographs of each of us:
Dieter, years younger, sulking next to an oversize barbell;
a clean-shaven Reuben, clenched and grimacing; Marina
in her spangles and smile; even me, pushing a broom,
eyes half-closed.

"I used to be thinner," Dieter said, squinting at the
page as it printed.

"Eck. There goes our plan." Valentino removed the
tasseled hat and wrung it in his hands. "If they've got our
photos, they'll surely recognize us, uniforms or no."

"Oh, come on," Marina replied. "We simply need to
do a more thorough job of disguising ourselves." She held
up a tin of shoe polish. "For example—we just smear this
on our faces, and voilà!"

"Voilà, we'll look like ourselves with shoe polish on
our faces, infant," Kovacsz said. "At best, you'll have dis-
guised yourself as yourself after eating a donut made of
feces."

Marina had already begun applying the shoe polish in
a ring around her mouth. Kovacsz was right, unfortunately.

"Um, if I may direct your attention over here?" Reuben said from the corner, not directing anyone's attention.

"I've got it," Valentino said, stretching a cord around

his head. "We use these rubber bands to distort our features, make us look older. The old guard. Nobody questions the elderly, right?" The band snapped into Valentino's eyes, and Martin yelped in sympathy.

"Everyone?" said Reuben. "What about—"

"Maybe this?" Bruce said, pulling a box of beige codpieces from a drawer. "We put these over our faces so that we look like Kloboukniks."

"And feast on pubic hair and crotch fleas. Fantastic plan," Kovacsz snorted.

"If only one of us could thoroughly disguise themselves, but unusually quickly," Sharon said, kicking at the thick pile of the lounge rug. "You know, deform their shape or alter their features or . . ."

"Please . . . everyone . . . if you wouldn't . . . mind . . . turning your heads . . . this way . . ." I turned to see Reuben crouched in the corner, naked to his undershorts, his face red as a tedfruit, every muscle and tendon quivering. Little bits of foam bubbled at the corners of his mouth as his cheeks began darkening with sharp nubs of stubble.

"Reuben," Kovacsz said, "your skills are truly impressive, and we do appreciate the effort, but we can't wait a whole day for you to grow your accursed beard. This is an urgent situation, demanding urgent solutions, not novelty acts that—" He stopped abruptly. In the time it had taken him to speak, Reuben had already generated a full goatee.

"The pain will be . . . considerable . . . tomorrow," Reuben barked, eyes shut tight, his jaw trembling with

effort between each word, "but . . . for Zloty . . . I shall enter . . . *overdrive*." The hair popped and slithered through
his pores, transforming him from boulevard dandy to
bristly park ranger as we stood gaping.

This was it. We had a mission, and we had a disguise.
Now all we needed was a leader—or an assistant ringmaster, at least. I was finally ready.

"Okay, here's the plan," I said, turning to the group.
"We dress Reuben up as a guard. We become his prisoners, who he has heroically captured in the corridors. He
parades us to the cell, locks us in with Zloty, snags the
key, and sends the other guards away to inform the supe-
riors. Once they're gone, he lets us all out, we give Zloty
a hug, and then run down the stairs. We'll be in Burford
by dinnertime."

"Burford?" said Kovacsz. "I am not going back to that
place."

"Fine—then Dupton, or Spagg, or the sandy beaches
of Fatkis Mudpit—wherever!" We heard another set of
clomping boots from below. "For now let's just *move*.
Someone find something to tie us up with."

I hardly recognized my own voice, but they leapt
into action. Dieter dug a chain out of a supply cabinet
while Reuben put on the uniform. We wrapped the chain
around our wrists so that we appeared to be firmly shack-
led, and Reuben pushed open the hatch, now sporting the
topiary of an old sea captain.

We shuffled out of the lounge and then through the

steel door that led to the prison block. The sloping walls of the cylindrical corridor were freshly plastered with over-size printouts of our photos, all of us in a row, again and again. We clinked along together, mute and united, as our names echoed over the loudspeaker. I was nervous, yes, but it was a good nervous, the nervousness that comes just before something amazing.

At the end of the hall a young bespectacled guard stood at attention in front of a cell. And there, through the bars of the door, was Zloty, still wearing the stupid top hat. Beneath the crusty brim, his eyes went wide at the sight of us.

"Underling!" Reuben shouted at the guard, who blushed as he jerked up even straighter. "It is I, your superior from an elite squad. A squad too elite for you to even know about. In fact, forget that I have even mentioned the squad. The important thing is that I have captured the diabolical ne'er-do-wells! Give me the keys to that cell." Reuben impatiently brushed aside his beard, which was now hermit-length, and reached out a hand.

"The ne'er-do-wells? You've captured them?" The guard looked at us one by one, comparing us to the photos on the wall. "That big one seems to have gotten even bigger."

Dieter sighed, which rattled the chains, sending the guard back to full attention.

"Well, for a man of his size, his metabolism is— soldier, I don't have time for this discussion. These

dangerous criminals belong behind bars. Givf me thrs"—
Reuben's mustache was curling as it grew, forcing its way
into his mouth. He frantically swiped it clear, spattering
the guard's face with a mist of saliva. "Give me those
kedth. The keephsth. The keys!"

"Of course, yes, of course!" said the guard. From
his belt he handed Reuben a single small key on a very
large ring.

"You shall be commended for thiths, myth gooth
mfn." Reuben carefully fit the key into the lock. The cell
door opened and there we were, face-to-face with Zloty.
His smile grew wider and wider as Reuben led us one by
one into the cell.

I tried to remain calm, to look morose and captured,
but inside I was soaring. We had done it. All of us, and
now even me. We had juggled and contorted and dodged
and smashed. We had schemed and believed and now the
scheme was becoming reality.

"Right, that's that," said Reuben, shutting the door
with a dramatic flourish. "The nation is safe. Young man,
go tell your commander that the uprising has been rebuffed. Better yet, why not take a fifteen- or twenty-minute
break, after all you've been through just now, and *then* go
tell your commander. But definitely go away from here."
Reuben turned to gesture down the corridor but stopped
abruptly, wincing. Keeping his head very still, he slid his
eyes back to our cell. I followed his gaze to the heavy iron
door, which had closed on his curtain of beard.

"Ah, cranberries," he said. "I seem to have accidentally—my beard—ha ha—let me just open—" He turned the key in the lock and yelped in pain. "It now appears that, well, my beard has become ensnarled in the locking mechanism. Young man, you wouldn't happen to have a cutting device of some kind that you could lend me before you run off?"

"Sir, do you mean to suggest that you are going to use a device to cut yourself free from this cell door, a device that I provide to you in advance, sir?"

"Yes, that is roughly what I had in mind."

"Sir, I cannot allow that to happen, sir."

Reuben stomped dramatically. "Soldier, I'll have you brought before a tribunal if you don't procure for me a nice sharp—"

"Sir, may I remind you of 12.36.c, sir? 'A uniformed guard must never allow a ranking officer to cut his or her own hair, nails, or vegetables.' Sir."

Reuben paused, biting his lip. "Well, yes, of course. Of course I know the law! But you see, this situation, with its urgency and potential danger, seems to me—"

The guard leaned in and squinted at Reuben's beard, and then at the cell's lock. "Sir, I have some bad news. A straight cut will simply not do. We're going to have to shave the entire beard."

"What? Isn't that—I mean, with these dangerous criminals . . ."

"12.36.d, sir—'Any guard who is responsible for the

aforementioned barbering must ensure that the results conform with current hygienic and cosmetological trends.' A crude snip job? With your head shape? Trust me on this, sir; in my boyhood I barbered upon my entire village. We must shave it clean."

"But how about you *first* cut the beard free in a single, heroic slash, and then *later* we can deal with the tidying and the code-meeting and whatnot? Perhaps this evening, or next week?"

But the guard had already begun lathering Reuben's beard with thick cream. He produced a pearl-handled razor from his utility belt. "There's no need to be worried—I have an extremely steady hand."

Reuben froze, trapped between the razor and the steel door. I watched them through the bars of the cell, unable to help or even breathe. The guard leaned in and lifted the razor with careful hands, resting its blade gently against Reuben's cheek. There was a long quiet moment, followed by a graceful shearing motion that left Reuben's chin as smooth as a peeled yam. "You do seem to know your way around a man's face," he said softly.

"This moment here is a great blessing," the guard replied, sliding the razor across Reuben's jawline with surgical precision. "It is my chance to do the thing I love most in the world." The blade glinted as the guard leaned close for a series of quick, delicate strokes. "And now . . . I am . . . *done*." He looked at Reuben to admire his work. "Ah, very good. I must say you are a handsome man under all that—" He squinted. "Not just handsome, but . . . familiar. Where have I seen you before? Perhaps we frequent the same haberdasher?"

The guard tilted his head, then wiped his spectacles and put them back on. Reuben stood against the cell door, smooth-faced and frozen. Next to him on the wall was the same clean-shaven visage, large as life. The guard squinted yet again, and now slowly lifted the razor, holding it out in front of him like a rapier. Reuben smiled weakly as his cheeks began to bloom with a fresh crop of stubble.

DAY EIGHT

"MAD AND JEALOUS AND HORNY."

by Hank Hamper - The Daily Scrutinizer

I told you, and I told them, and now the telling has become the showing: a gaggle of weepy, wimpy faces peering through our prison bars. I can't literally *show* you the faces, of course, for security reasons, but I assure you: Weepy. Wimpy. And most important, *thwarted*.

Yes, the criminal action has been thwarted. Thwarted, cornered, slapped, shoved up against a few crumbly walls, and thrown headlong into Kornblatt's cell, where they now sit, thinking their last thoughts, praying their final prayers to whatever chubby god they worship. Citizens, you can now safely return to your regularly scheduled lives. Play a vigorous round of badminton with your nephews, eat table grapes from a crystal bowl, do your bathroom business without fear or embarrassment—because the threat, my friends, has been eliminated. Yesterday the mister. Today the Kornblatts. Tomorrow . . . well, tomorrow I shall reach for the greatest prize of them all. It's a new era of results, of follow-through, of actions and consequences.

Just as I forecast, the plan worked to perfection, luring the attackers closer and closer, fueling the fires of hope—which is the hottest fire there be, and also the most deadly, for the fire of hope is all warmth and no light, drawing the frostbitten seekers closer and closer while still shrouded in darkness, until they stumble into the flames themselves and are consumed. Or hurled into a jail cell alongside their stupid leader with the dandy's hat.

Yes, you should have seen those hopeful faces! And how quickly the hope fled, the moment it was confronted with reality, the crushing reality of our crushing power. Let this be a lesson: The system works. Do not fight the system. Do not object. Do not dither and dather and hem and haw. Don't whine, don't sulk, don't gripe, don't grope. Again: *The system works.* That's why they call it a system! Every piece must function correctly, and every citizen has a role to play: sharing delicious recipes, completing relevant paperwork, whatever. And now these criminals have played theirs—the grain of irritating sand that allows the oyster to make a beautiful pearl. The oyster is our nation, of course, and the pearl is all this very cool stuff you see around you: the artisanal market, jazz in the park, chicken finger Fridays. Kornblatt and his ring of antisocial miscreants may be dirty and weepy and wimpy, and they may hate you and want to take away your chicken fingers and do you harm (sick kinds of harm involving eye contact and awkward dance moves), but still: everything in its place. We didn't even have to go fetch them—they helpfully put themselves in exactly the right spot, marked by the satisfying click of the cell door closing behind them.

And that's where they are now, ready for Kornblatt's starring role in tomorrow's festivities. They can even peer out the cell's window—it's a bit narrow and cobwebby, and little birds fly around and try to peck your eyes out, but hopefully they can still see the stage upon which he will deliver his final performance. I am referring, of course, to the Termination Field, our laboratory of consequences, our monument to democracy. Members of the Uniformed Youth have outfitted the field with all possible tools of correction: gallows, firing squad, various electrified furnishings, flesh-eating parasites, bees, beads, traumatized primates, common allergens, etc.—all citizen-suggested, justice-approved.

This may seem excessive, but I feel it is necessary. Decisions like this are too weighty to be handed down from above; the people, in their amassed wisdom, must determine the method of execution. I have my own opinions, of course, but I won't attempt to influence this sacred process. Each individual citizen has the right—and the responsibility—to choose for him or herself from the many wonderful options, all on display and at the ready in the Termination Field. What's more, devices can be combined in pairs or trios to allow the punishment to most precisely fit the criminal. Are you going to start out with the Disorienting Luge, then the Parasite Time Machine, ending in the Cavern of Mirror Shards? Or is that too artsy for you? Maybe you'd prefer to just link up three pummelers in a row? This event is all about self-expression! Well, 60 percent about self-expression, 40 percent about justicing a bunch of dirty-faced fearmongers.

Of course, it can be difficult to pick just a single punishment—and so our thoughtful leaders have helpfully scheduled eight extra executions. Yesterday evening, after a highly efficient trial, Kornblatt's kohorts were convicted of various crimes—falsified permits, destruction of government lasers, beard fraud—and space was found in tomorrow's already-crowded schedule. (The canine has been sentenced merely to life imprisonment in one of those head-cone things; never let it be said that we are not merciful.)

So it seems that tomorrow afternoon will be the final "performance" of this "circus." I am using those quote marks because they never really were a circus at all, of course. And they won't actually be performing, obviously—they'll be double-guarded, constantly watched, just in case anyone has any stupid glimmers of hints of whispers of dreams of escaping. It's not going to happen, so don't even think about it.

Unfortunately, the ceremony's scheduled host, our beloved Chet Choochy, has fallen prey to sudden gastrointestinal distress (he seemed so healthy just yesterday, when I stopped by his dressing room to drop off a congratulatory gift basket of aged oysters and warm mayo). Choochy's replacement, I am embarrassed and honored to report, is one Hank Hamper—an honor surely not deserved, but who am I to decline the call? They say I have a face for radio and a voice for newspapers, ha ha, so please don't be frightened, ha ha. Do I deserve an honor of this magnitude? Debatable. Will I let you down with bush-league punnery and vaudeville propwork? Not a chance. I will host to my very hostliest, attempting to meet the demands of this most sacred of days—and then I may just add a little finale of my own. What an unimaginably perfect occasion for someone to publicly, heroically declare his affections for another, if someone were cunning enough to seize such an opportunity.

Objectivity, of course, is the ideal and responsibility of any journalist, and I have tried to hold to that throughout the stressful and ultimately triumphant events of the past week. But, now that the trials are all over, I can finally admit it: I hate these guys. I hate their stupid outfits and wimpy faces and dumb circus gimmick, and I know you hate them, too—we all do! Everyone, that is, but one person: Madame J. That woman, in her cosmic grace, seems to know no hate. She will—it makes me so mad to type this, so mad and jealous and horny—Madame J will even be paying the agitators a special visit in their cell tomorrow morning, a benediction and final reckoning before the festivities. A mission of mercy or understanding or something—I don't even know. We must *communicate*, she says, even with those who seem beyond our understanding, those who are so unlike us. The thought of those sickos inhaling her shimmering presence for up to twenty minutes, while those of us who labor ceaselessly for our nation in hopes that someday they may share a bowl of mixed berries . . . No—I must stay calm. I must be patient, for just one more day. One more day of solitude, one final day of loneliness and longing.

Tomorrow the citizens of our nation will assemble outside the Confinement Needle. Tomorrow we shall be united once again. But, of course, we've been together all along—joined by the golden threads of the Pickle Index, the vibrant skein of our shared culinary heritage, from krauts to cornichons. Some have said the Index is obsolete, outdated, a vestigial remnant of a simpler time. Some have fretted the recipes are no longer even read—or worse, not even valid *recipes*. Seriously? Some sick loner, going to all that trouble just to pollute the home-fermentation community with moody ramblings? And even if, who would ever want to read such a thing? Not a chance, I say. I say, the Index is more vital than ever. I say, that simpler time is still with us, *within* us. We are knitted together more tightly than ever, and tomorrow we shall unfurl that brine-soaked tapestry for all to see.

Well, that's the news for today. I've got to get to the florist before they close. And you, dear readers, Destinians and Burfordites and Plolos alike, need to purchase your tickets to the festivities. Really, please do this, as it's a lot of fun and also mandatory. Tomorrow morning, Madame J will communicate. Tomorrow evening, the rest of us will have our chance.

RECIPE NAME
[Rotted Cabbage]

INGREDIENTS

[Head of cabbage; dirty bathtub or slop-trough; three days]

INSTRUCTIONS

They shoved Reuben into the cell with the rest of us. He crashed against the plank that served as Zloty's one piece of furniture—unless you counted the slop bucket as a piece of furniture—and slid down the wall into a heap, the final casualty of my failed caper. Apparently I couldn't be satisfied with my standard irrelevance; no, I had to offer a brilliant plan that brought us directly into the jail cell.

Zloty sat on the far end of the plank, legs crossed, thin as a whipfish in his prison smock and top hat. He scanned the room, gazing silently at each of us, and then lowered his head into his hands. His shoulders began to heave, and Marina reached out to comfort him, but then realized that he was shuddering with laughter.

"Reuben," he said, his eyes bright with tears, "that was amazing! The beard-in-the-door bit—marvelous. You should really consider incorporating that into your act."

"I, well," said Reuben, rubbing his cheek where it had struck the wall, "it didn't go entirely as planned. But perhaps there were aspects worth retaining, yes, I can see that."

"Without a doubt!" said Zloty. "It will fit perfectly into a new show I've been developing this past week. An extravaganza, really. I have all your parts planned out in my head. And I've concocted a whole new routine for the finale. A bit of magic, some self-puppetry, plus a few new elements that I can't discuss in this setting. A grand garbanzo for the head and heart. Your hair skills plus my clownery—it can't miss!"

"Um, Zloty?" said Kovacsz. "Who's your audience for this extravaganza—the guards?"

"Believe me, I've tried." He frowned. "They don't seem to have much of a sense of humor, to be honest."

"And when are you planning to debut it? Before, after, or during the execution?"

"Right, the execution," said Zloty. "They tell me it's tomorrow." He turned to Reuben. "Which means we have a lot of work to do!"

"What we need to be working on," said Dieter, "is getting out of here."

Zloty put his hand on my shoulder. "I am so happy to see all of you. Really. It has been so lonely in here, just me and this slop bucket, which I have named Yamtam. So I am truly thankful to have you here, and I can only imagine what struggles you endured along the way. But as for getting out of here"—he paused to rub some grime from his chin—"I am afraid that there is nothing to be done."

"Ah," Valentino said, "but that is where you are wrong, Mr. Kornblatt!" Even Martin Van Buren squinted at Valentino as he leapt to his feet, a finger waggling in the air. "Our group has overcome much worse than this simple prison cell, haven't we, my fragrant little cherry blossom?" The dog returned its attention to the slop bucket.

"Hmm," Dieter said, tapping a knuckle on the gray cell wall. "I'm sure I could burst through this stone fairly easily."

"Oh, the walls, I should mention—" said Zloty, raising a hand as Dieter threw his shoulder against the wall, which curled in around him, absorbing his body like thick caramel. "They're made of some material that gets softer and stickier the more force you apply to it."

Kovacsz squatted to examine a small circular grate in the corner of the cell. "If I can somehow wedge myself . . . ," he said, collapsing his shoulders and squeezing his head through the hole.

"Oh, you don't want to go down there," said Zloty. "That vents the septic tank for the entire prison." We heard a muffled retch, and Kovacsz pulled his head out of the floor, gagging.

Valentino sighed, gripping the door's iron bars.

"Unfortunately, Martin is quite incompetent when it comes to lock picking."

And then there was nothing left to say. Marina sat on the plank next to Zloty, who put his arm around her. "But listen, my friends," he said, pausing to cough a strand of green phlegm into the slop bucket. "You made it this far! I never guessed that such a ragged assortment of scoot-mongers and dill-snippers could sneak yourselves into a kraut-pouch, much less a place like this. Come on now, tell me of your adventures."

Valentino cleared his throat and started at the beginning, detailing the final show in Burford, Moritz's arrival in our tent, Moritz's departure in the pickle barrel. Kovacsz contorted into his pose from the breadbread trunk, complete with furious thigh-scratching. Dieter re-mimed his wall miming. Marina stood against the cell wall and described each prong, dart, and shuriken that the black-clad assassin had thrown her way. The story stretched into the dawn, and through it all Zloty was rapt, smiling and laughing and gasping in all the right places. I squeezed next to him on the plank and felt warm. I remembered the first time I saw those striped tents, yellow and red and blue against the dead brown hills, and then the show that night, every minute of it, my hands still stained with farm-dirt, my eyes wide, my jaw open. Back then I thought they could do anything. I didn't belong, but I felt lucky just to be near.

The guard outside our cell snapped to attention.

We turned to see a procession of young boys in orange smocks pour into the corridor. One by one they lined each side of the hallway. A guard held the steel door at the far end and I braced myself for another visit from the prong thrower, or a troop of pointy-helmeted thugs swinging slumber clubs, or some new torment that I couldn't even imagine—but instead there was a long pause. Some kind of iridescent fog puffed into the hall, and suddenly I smelled strawberries. An organ chord boomed, echoing off the stone walls, and then Madame J rounded the corner.

She walked along the line of boys, stopping occasionally to smile or shake hands or compliment a well-ironed smock. The octopus was cradled under her left arm, just like in the murals. I'd somehow assumed it was a metaphorical octopus, although I'm not sure what the metaphor would have been—the many arms of justice, the tenacious suckercups of liberty? But there it was, in all its literal glory, a glistening shadow casting its tentacles across her long white shawl. On her feet were simple ballet slippers, which were nearly silent except for a papery whisper each time she slid her bad leg along the stone floor. We all watched, mesmerized, as she approached the cell. Pad, whisper. Pad, whisper. Pad, whisper.

And then she was at our door. I'd always thought the paintings and photos were exaggerated, airbrushed—but now I saw the images for the crude scribbles they were. Even in this decrepit prison cell, surrounded by glowering guards, probably sentenced to death or worse, I somehow felt better, warmer, safer in her presence.

A guard unlocked the door and opened it.

"Hello, everyone," Madame J said, stepping across the threshold into our cell. "Sorry about all that nonsense—they insist on making such a fuss. How was your night?"

Reuben opened his mouth, then closed it, then opened it again. Dieter rubbed his elbow. No one spoke.

She smiled. "Well, I wouldn't expect you to be jumping for joy. It is a sad day for all of you. Well, not as sad as tomorrow, I suppose!" She surveyed the room. "I thought you might be feeling a little distressed, and so I thought I'd stop by to offer some perspective on your situation. After all, the example you will provide to citizens everywhere will be invaluable. Yes, you'll all die terribly, painfully, in some severely humiliating fashion, witnessed by a crowded, eager stadium—but each one of those countrymen will remember you. Each one will carry you in their heads and in their hearts and think, 'I will never do to my nation what these poor souls did.' And they never will. They will find their amusement in proper venues, and they will provide entertainment only after appropriate certification. They will learn from *your* mistakes. I think that's pretty impressive."

She turned to face Zloty, the white shawl swaying behind her. I found myself worrying that it would touch the cell walls.

"I don't want you to feel guilty or ashamed, Mr.

Kornblatt," she said. "A country is like a child. If a child scrapes his knee, we must wash it thoroughly to clear out germs, to prevent infection. We don't blame the child. We don't even blame the germs. We cherish them all, each in their own way." She scanned our faces. "Are any of you parents? No? Let me try again." She thought for a moment, stroking the octopus's smooth mantle. "Think of our nation as a theater. You had a role to play, and you played it. You all did. The villain is as necessary as the hero—maybe more so. I don't even like to use that word, *villain*. Our nation is a nation of heroes. Even you. *Especially* you, because it is you who will sacrifice the most. On behalf of our people and all who have come before, I thank you. I thank you all." She smiled, and the octopus curled a dark tentacle around her left wrist. "Tomorrow, the people will thank you as well, in their own way. Not so pleasant, perhaps, but no less heartfelt. You will feel their gratitude upon your bodies and bones."

And then she was gone, the white shawl disappearing into a sea of orange smocks.

Zloty tilted his head and rubbed his hands together slowly. Dieter blinked hard, as if he were waking from a dream. Martin Van Buren folded himself onto the stone floor and sighed. I didn't move.

DAY NINE

"YOUR DESIGN, YOUR VOTE, YOUR WHIM."

by Hank Hamper - The Daily Scrutinizer

The festivities are upon us! In the misty hours just past dawn, the Termination Field is silent, church-like, golden and glowing as light slants through the early fog. And looming through the luminous gray, massive and ancient as the dinosaurs, rise the many fingers of justice: The Inverted Gallows. The Pit of Toasty Stones. The Wall of Bees & Wallabies. They are otherworldly and inscrutable, like some vine-covered temple from mythic times, and yet oddly familiar, our dear old friends. And, indeed, how many times before have we come together, our people and these living monuments, united in this holy celebration of our nation's ideals?

In the center of these structures sits an empty stage, somehow more vivid for its lack of blade or rope or snarling beast. It is on that stage I now sit, cross-legged and utterly alone, ringed by empty bleachers, the worn wooden planks. Tonight those bleachers will be overflowing with spectators, and tonight this stage will present the true stars of the show. For the moment they snooze in their cell up above, troubled only by their consciences. Soon, though, they may find their troubles more . . . tangible.

But *which* of these glorious machines shall be selected to deliver tonight's justice? That is the question bandied from citizen to citizen, from scroller to scroller. Which stately implement has been deemed best suited for the particularities of each crime, each criminal? Well, my lips are sealed—you'll just have to wait till tonight.

For now all I will say is: Bravo. Bravo to you, dear readers, for your collective spirit, for your ingenuity, for your pluck. After all, these machines were built according to *your* design, *your* vote, *your* whim. I even overheard some of the tech guys here marveling at what an impressive array you've brought together. These guys don't just hand out compliments like a chipmeister at a nacho party, okay? They lead serious, monastic lives, dedicated pretty much exclusively to issues of execution and execution-related maintenance. On top of that, remember that I *overheard* them in the washroom. They gave this praise to you, dear readers, not knowing that they were "on the record." So be proud. You have created something beautiful, and soon you will have your reward.

* * *

By noon the sun is high and hot, and crowds are amassing at the gates, eager to claim spots with the best view of the action. They've flocked from all corners, from Grütn and Burford and Ploly, all yearning to make their voices heard. Finally the doors open, and in they rush: young families carrying fat babies and large umbrellas; old soldiers in their dusty, tasseled regalia; robust teens still recounting favorite moments from last year's ceremony. Some grill traditional fare—skewered rodents, charred nut-meat— while others line up at the refreshment stands to buy batter-fried wolf eggs, duck-fat hoagies, and rice-encrusted choadlers. Migrant barkers shout through greased cones, and a man in a skeleton suit hands out free snifters of bone dust.

But this feast of hoagies and choadlers only sharpens our thirst—the thirst to set wrongs right, to extinguish fear and thereby learn courage, to tie all loose threads into one tidy knot. Citizens stroll among the implements of termination, examining the machinery, taking measurements and testing blades. Fathers and sons, like so many fathers and sons before them, debate the pros and cons of each apparatus, the traditional and the new-fangled alike. "But Dad," I overhear, "couldn't the toxin diffusion delay the death-confirmation procedures?" Our precocious youth! Another chubby lad pipes up: "I like the pointy parts." Me too, son, me too.

In the Animalia quadrant, the shark tank sloshes into the mamba pit, eliciting an angry chorus of hisses. In the

Viral aisle, vendors sell hairless mice dressed in tiny prison stripes to citizens who'd like to test the smorgasbord of spores.

And high above it all dangles the presentation pod, the glass egg wherein our ten guests must wait and quiver until tonight's starring role. I can see them now, an ugly bunch huddled in the egg's rounded base. Each is outlandishly yucky in a different way—odd body shapes, unfashionable styling, mange—but all are consumed in the same private sorrows, eyes downcast or closed tight. All except one, a young woman or elderly girl, who is staring out the curved glass, looking my way. Our eyes meet. She is outlandish here only for her relative blandness—clean enough, a bit underfed, with an aura of perpetual defeat. Well, you won't have to worry about that anymore, darling. Just one final downfall, and then your tedious story will be at its welcome end.

She blinks, then looks away. I wonder what she's thinking, what she's feeling. Remorse? Shame? Or are they still plotting the overthrow of—you know what? I actually *don't* wonder, not anymore. They had their chance to be interesting and respectable, and they blew it all on hopped-up, half-baked, ill-founded hatemongering.

So let them get ravaged by the sand badgers—I don't care! Maybe when their bones are turning to soup in the Harmimal they'll understand the . . . Oh, my goodness, did I just mention two of the machines we'll be using tonight? Crumbs! You didn't just hear that, dear readers, did you? About the Sand Badger Bonanza and the Harmimal, a mouthy-looking apparatus that softens victims' bones to the consistency of pancake batter? Oh, fractals—I've just mentioned them again! Guess the cat's out of the bag on these two, folks. But fear not—there are still seven more implements of perfect termination waiting to be unveiled at tonight's extravaganza. Patience.

As afternoon turns to dusk, the chatter settles into a thoughtful murmur. If it's true, as they say, that a country without an engaged populace is like a body with no spleen, then our glorious nation must be the most splenetic of all. Just look at this turnout! The citizens understand that their role in today's events is both vital and sacred; unanimity is the concrete slab from which our nation's spires erupt, and so all opinions must be given time to congeal into one. We will then bring out the prisoners to receive the specifics of their sentences, a different solution for each problematic individual—and then the main event will begin.

I am ready.

Ready for the ceremony, of course, and also ready for my own contribution, my special communiqué, my declaration of eternal love. Ready for the rest of my life to begin—ready to truly *live*. I'm not going to go into all the details at the moment, but let's just say that some of the following elements might be involved: a boutonniere of thorny moonblossom, which happens to be the Madame's favorite flower, its tiny razor-pricks nestled beneath a cloud of ghostly beauty; a tearaway cummerbund, adorned with mesmerizing sequined spirals; and the sheet music for "My Eyes Were Empty Holes Till I Filled Them with You," a song of my own composition. I have informed the security staff that there might be certain unscheduled twists added to the festivities, and that they are not to interfere with anything that happens, regardless of how surprising or heartwarming or erotic it becomes.

Wish me luck, citizens! I will give it my all, and you will surely give it your all, and then we will give them their all.

RECIPE NAME

[Jar]

INGREDIENTS

[One jar (empty); failure]

INSTRUCTIONS

It was difficult to tell what was happening on the stage—the glass sphere we were in made everything look flat and melted, and the announcer's voice was muffled by the roaring of the crowd. But we had a perfect overhead view of the contraptions they had designed for our executions, which they paraded across the entire length of the field. Isolated in the sphere, so high up, I felt weirdly peaceful, even as the guards wheeled out the hulking machines, a blur of spinning blades, heat tubes, jackal tanks, and bone witherers. There was nothing more to be done, no more secret skills or unexpected heroics. There was nothing left to do but watch the show.

"And for Dieter Brakconner," the smiling announcer

said, waving at the screen behind him, which showed a picture of Dieter from his military days, "we have developed something very, very special." The announcer was a healthy-looking, square-toothed man wearing a shiny black suit with a floppy white flower in the lapel. He walked to a lever at the base of a large platform holding a flesh-colored dummy. "They say he is a strongman, but tonight we will put this claim to the test. This is, of course, a simulation— keep your eye on the dummy!" The announcer pulled the lever and a boulder came sailing out of the sky. I cringed, expecting the dummy to be pulverized, but instead the boulder smashed into the cantilevered edge of the platform, sending the figure in a high arc across the stage. It crashed through a series of electrified metal plates and into the open throat of a large metallic tube full of mating locusts. The dummy made its way down through the tube, dropping into a tank filled with pressurized gas that rendered the inhaler intensely bored.

"Obviously, this will have no effect on the dummy, who is already very bored with all this," the announcer said. "But no weight training could prepare a strongman for such paralytic ennui!" The dummy was then spit out onto a conveyor lined with reformatory boys wielding cups of nettles picked out of the dung of forest wolves. By the time it got to the pore-expanding wind tunnel, the dummy was little more than a mound of flesh-colored pulp.

"Looks just like you, old boy," Kovacsz said, slapping Dieter on the shoulder.

"I do not like nettles," said Dieter.

They rolled the Dieter contraption off the stage and brought on Marina's device, which consisted of a gurney dangling from a cigar-shaped balloon. "This cunning rogue narrowly avoided death from the prongman's prongs. But can she avoid a prong*storm*?"

"Eh," Marina said, "I could probably avoid that, actually."

"I don't want to see mine," Reuben said, turning away as they wheeled out a bathtub full of steroidal lice.

"Everyone, listen to me," Zloty said. "I do not want any of you to worry. I have a plan."

"Please, no more about your performance, Zloty," Kovacsz said. "I would like to spend my last minutes on this earth thinking about fine ladies and sea air and golden bathtubs, undisturbed and unclowned."

Zloty smiled. "Trust me, my friend. I have been studying these people for the past week. I know them inside out. I know exactly what makes them—"

We never got to hear the end of Zloty's speech, because just then the glass sphere was released onto a long wide track that curved toward the stage. The sphere rolled steadily along the track, but the glass interior was so frictionless that we were able to sit in place and watch the audience as we passed over their heads. Martin Van Buren whined and buried his head in Valentino's crotch. Brassy music blared over the loudspeakers, warped and lopsided inside the tumbling sphere.

We docked in a cavity at the center of the stage. The announcer came forward and put his hand on the glass. "In just moments, my friends," he said to the crowd, "your fears will be withered, nettled, and pulped. We do it all for you." A man in an orange jumpsuit approached with a blowtorch and began cutting a circular hatch in the sphere.

"Remember, I will take care of this," Zloty said, stepping forward so that he could exit the sphere first.

"You mean take care of getting us all killed?" Kovacsz replied.

"I'm pretty sure that's already been arranged," Bruce said. Sharon pantomimed Bruce being serviced by a mountain goat, but her heart didn't seem in it. I tried to tell myself that this was just another twist in the caper, nothing to worry about, despite the distinct sensation that my head was exploding.

Zloty gave us that familiar crooked smile and held up his hand for silence. The torchman completed the circle and applied a suction handle to the outer surface. With a single tug the glass came free.

"Guards, please fetch the prisoners," the announcer said, and four heavily tasseled men came forward with shatterbolts. But Zloty stepped through the opening before they could even enter. He extended his foot gracefully onto the stage, shifting his weight expertly so that he landed in a perfect posture of genuflection. Then he rose, arms extended like a conductor before an orchestra, eyes shut tight.

"Behold the ringleader, the fomenter of terror, the fermenter of fear! The furrier of farce if farce were a fur!" the announcer proclaimed. "He sought nothing less than domination and subjugation, but now, thanks to the Madame's grace, his schemes have been neutralized, nullified, nipped." The announcer paused, then smiled and slid the white blossom from his lapel. "Speaking of our divine Madame J, I would like to take this opportunity to say a few words of my own." He turned to her reserved box, just offstage, and took a deep breath. "Madame, a journalist is most fundamentally an *observer*, and thus I have had the distinct honor of witnessing your daily triumphs from this unique vantage. But I am not just a journalist—I am also a *man*, and a man can merely observe for only so long. And so I am now here to declare . . . or, well, to sweetly implore . . . I mean, what I'm trying to say is—"

At that moment, Zloty clapped his hands and dropped into something approximating a full split. He then splayed his fingers on the stageboards and lifted himself by his arms, legs still thrust outward, so that he seemed to be levitating, sort of.

The Termination Field went silent.

Zloty began to walk on his hands toward the announcer, grunting slightly with the effort but keeping his smile big and bright. The announcer stared at him with bewildered shock, helplessly spluttering at the interruption. Zloty seized the moment, springing to his feet and plucking the large flower from the dazed man's hand. He held it aloft, and I gasped: I had seen this before, in one of Zloty's books, one of his favorites—*Transmigrational Strategies for Plant & Beast*. He had shown me one night after all the others had gone to sleep. "Very interesting," he'd said, tapping the page. "Very . . . insouciant." I remember the woodcut diagram of a flower being placed into a mouth, at just the precise angle, and then on the following page the reveal: a tiny bird fluttering out through open, smiling lips. "Functional with any standard smooth-stemmed bloom," Zloty said. "Suitable for all ages. I am impressed." He chuckled to himself and carefully copied the illustrations into his notebook.

Now, onstage, he displayed the flower to the mass of spectators beyond the spotlights, and then to the announcer, who seemed to be on the verge of tears. And then, with a single flick of the wrist, Zloty popped it into his mouth, stem and all. Still no one spoke. He faced the audience, his index finger hovering in the air. He waited a moment, rotating his jaw, bobbing his Adam's apple, pursing his lips. And then he smiled a broad, closed-mouth smile. And then smiled some more, and then some more. And it was on that third round of smiles that I knew something was wrong.

Zloty snapped his fingers and opened his mouth wide, but no bird fluttered out. Instead, he broke into a deep, rasping retch. He bent at the waist and held his ribs and coughed and coughed. Finally something seemed to catch, and a small wad of soggy petals shot from his mouth, landing on the announcer's shiny black wingtips. He coughed once more, and a crumpled, thorny stem drifted down to the stage. Zloty looked up, gave a weak smile, and wiped his eyes, his shoulders still heaving with deep breaths.

Aside from his panting, the stadium was silent once again. The wet petals glistened in the spotlight. Then, from somewhere out beyond the stage, I heard a familiar noise—a long, rattling wheeze that gave way to a percussive sideways cackle. I squinted through the darkness and caught her distinctive silhouette in the third row: Mrs. Tralm, the stoic pride of Burford, shuddering with laughter. Her sons stood behind her, each gripping a handle of the wheelchair. Someone else chuckled, and then a ripple ran through the crowd, giggles and snorts and even a few guffaws. The sounds grew and reverberated through the stadium, small shadowy heads undulating in staggered waves. A voice yelled, "Oh, no, he's going to terrorize our nation's floral arrangements!" Someone else shouted, "What, he'll kill us with his jazz hands?" The heckling gathered strength, cresting into an indistinguishable roar. My breath caught in my throat.

The announcer whispered something to one of the guards, and a moment later a thunderous burst of feedback erupted from the loudspeakers, so loud and low that it rattled our teeth. The buzz decayed into crackles, and then the only sound was a pattering of stifled cries from the children's brigade.

The announcer looked out over the crowd. He lifted the microphone to his face and smiled a tepid half-smile. "Thank you," he said, "for your cooperation. These termination machines are, of course, quite dangerous, and so we need absolute silence and unanimous support to ensure that they harm only their intended harmees. The locusts are effective, but so . . . distractible. And so very hungry." He walked forward, grimacing briefly as he stepped on the slick mess of petals Zloty had spit up. "And now—let the ceremonies begin."

He raised an arm, and two large men stepped toward Zloty. I heard Dieter sobbing behind me, and Kovacsz buried his face in Martin's fur.

"Stop," I said. "Just . . . stop." I don't remember stepping out through the hole in the glass sphere, and even now it sounds like a terrible idea, but there I was, onstage, face-to-face with the guards, who froze in confusion at the sight of me. I felt like I was watching myself from the outside, from miles away and years before, peering through the flaps of an old canvas tent. To keep talking was like tumbling into a nightmare, but it was better than the alternative. I looked out at the black void beyond the footlights.

"Hey, you out there," I said, because I am so eloquent. "Everyone out there. I don't know who you are— well, I do see Mrs. Tralm from Burford, hi, hello"—she loosed a toothy whistle—"and you don't know me. But those questions you were shouting? You already know the answers. You know this man is no evil mastermind. He's not even a master clown—sorry, Zloty." The announcer was gesturing frantically toward me, but the guards hesitated, uncertain. "He can hardly run a circus, much less a revolution. What he can do is, he believes. He believes things into being. Even when all good sense would suggest the opposite. He believes a hair-growing man can be a featured attraction. He believes an elderly dog is as ferocious as a lion. He believes a dirt-prodding girl can . . ." I paused, trying to remember what the dirt-prodding girl was supposedly capable of.

The announcer came forward. "A dirt-prodding girl can be a volunteer for the night's first execution! Let's give a warm welcome to Flora Bialy while we unveil an audience favorite, the Holy Roller." He tucked the microphone under his arm and began applauding furiously, the claps echoing throughout the hushed arena. The pair of guards took me by each arm, but their hearts didn't seem in it.

A voice came from the darkened bleachers. "I, um, my friend accidentally heard about someone who might have read a, um, recipe that sounds, well, sort of a lot like that girl, and, well, I wonder if it's possible that those guys actually aren't really instigators or whatever?" Heads turned in all directions, trying to locate the speaker. "I mean, they don't even sound like very good circus people. According to my friend."

"You read what?" I called into the masses. "Which

girl? But, well, yes—you're right, we're not! Instigators, I mean. Or good circus people, I guess."

"I also might have heard about someone who got forwarded one of those same recipe things," another voice called out, "and I got the same feeling. Like, that big guy is big, but he doesn't even smash stuff."

Out across the field, I could hear a general murmuring, what sounded like mass agreement. Which was impossible, of course.

"You mean . . . both of you? That doesn't even make sense." I squinted out into the shadows. "Anyway, you're right, he doesn't! It's extremely frustrating."

"Well, I actually *read* them!" shouted a chubby man in the front row, gesturing wildly with a baton of cotton candy. "By yesterday it was like the only thing getting passed around the Index. And I can tell you: the wiry dude is a sourpuss, the spangle woman is basically unemployed, and that couple is still bickering about some nonsense from twenty years ago!"

Now the calls came from all over. "They don't even have a functioning smokepoot, the dunces!" Derisive snorts floated from distant bleachers. "That beard really is impressive, though." Reuben beamed through a thicket of bristles. "Is that dog dead? I think it might be dead."

Martin Van Buren had dropped into a deep sleep, legs splayed, tongue absently lapping at the stage.

"Certainly not!" said Valentino. "He's simply lying

in wait, conserving energy for a blood-curdling assault. I suggest that you do not agitate or—"

"Valentino, you're not helping," I hissed.

"And you, grouchy girl," someone else called out from the sea of shadowy heads, "you seem to construct a shell of passivity and skepticism as an attempt to protect yourself against possible disappointment."

"Well . . ."

"Also, I tried your cuke-fudge dippin' stix. My whole family did."

"Your family? My recipe? Really?"

"We were so excited, sitting around the table, clutching our stix, ready to dip." A long sigh. "That was the worst meal we ever had."

"Oh."

"We've had some pretty terrible meals, but that was a whole other level. Like, organ-failure bad."

"I'm sorry—I didn't realize anyone—"

"The house had to be fumigated. My husband left me the next day."

I still couldn't quite comprehend how or why these people knew us so well—my recipes? everybody?—but this was no time for questions. My job now was to keep the show rolling. I looked at Zloty, but he was just grinning. I breathed deep and stepped to the front of the stage.

"Those were terrible recipes, it's true, and we are a terrible circus, that's true too. But that's my point: you can see all this for yourselves, no matter what story they tell you. And it's not even a really great story, is it? The bad guys all die in the end, but you still go back to your pickles and smokepoots and sad, frightened lives."

"Ah, the futility," said Kovacsz, still sitting in the glass sphere. "Our little girl has finally seen the light!"

"And if someday you stop being frightened, there'll be a new bad guy and a new execution and you'll be entertained and frightened all over again. All this"—I waved my hand toward the stage, the announcer, the machines, the prison tower looming behind us—"this is the real circus, isn't it?" The crowd stared at me, mouths slightly agape; apparently I had lost them with my poetic analogy. I knew I didn't have much longer. "But you don't need to accept the circus you've been given—you can make your own. I mean, we did it, right? And look at *us*." I gestured behind me, where Zloty was still trying to pick bits of stem from his teeth. "So, ladies and gentlemen, step right up, step on forward! Witness feats, witness follies. Witness yourselves. Let's put on a show! Mrs. Tralm, how about you? What do you have for us?"

Mrs. Tralm's beefy sons hoisted her wheelchair onto the stage. She sat there grinning, and I felt a knifing panic as I realized that I'd staked our fate on a secret talent I was pretty sure Mrs. Tralm did not possess. She grabbed the chair's wheels and clenched her teeth. I clenched mine, too, trying to figure out where this was headed. The audience was riveted. Then, slowly, the front of the chair inched off the ground. She held this pop-a-wheelie for a moment, then clattered back to the stage. The arena erupted in applause.

Immediately, a young woman came scrambling over the edge of the stage. She still wore her work skirt from the dairy, and her cheeks were flushed with excitement. She turned her back to the audience, bent over, and began to lift her skirt. An eager hush spread throughout the crowd. There was a moment of silence, and then from her hindquarters came the warbling notes of a songbird. She followed this with an owl hoot and then a mighty eagle's cry, and the masses roared their approval.

Before the dairy worker could even pull her skirt back down, a skinny man in a red silk tuxedo was already standing in the spotlight. He held two loaves of bread-bread in one hand and a chain saw in the other, and a grinning baboon was nestled under his arm. The baboon took the loaves and leapt atop the man's head. The man tied a blindfold around his eyes, started the chain saw, and held it aloft. I didn't want to see, but I couldn't look away.

The announcer finally snarled an order at the guards, who had been standing next to me, lost in the spectacle, loosening their grip with each new feat. He pointed at them and then drew his finger menacingly across his throat, but boos rained down from every corner of the arena. "People, people!" said the announcer, turning to address them. "I enjoy a good show as much as the rest of you! Probably more so! But there's a time for shows and a time for bone withering! And, if I may clarify, this particular time happens to have been specifically designated for the latter!"

"Let's wither *his* bones!" someone shouted. The baboon threw a loaf of breadbread at the announcer, which exploded in a crumbly puff at his feet. He pawed blindly through the floury smoke, gasping and coughing, and then ran for the needle. The crowd came surging forward, a swirling tide of bodies. I couldn't see Dieter anymore, nor Marina, Bruce, Sharon, or any of the rest. I climbed the ladder of a free-fall tower and peered out over the joyful chaos. And finally I found Zloty, standing at the center of the whorling mass of people, just watching them with that crooked half-smile, that weird spark of hope. The announcer made it to the door of the needle moments ahead of a pack of kids armed with angry locusts, but then the red-tuxedoed man fired up the chain saw and all eyes turned back to the stage. The show went on.

DAY TEN

"A BROWN, FARTY, TOXIC CLOUD."

by Hank Hamper - The Daily Scrutinizer

In times of instability, the people look to their government to lead, the way a child will rush to a parent when
danger is near. And so it is understandable, dear readers, that so many of you would throng to the base of the
Confinement Needle, where we've set up a nimble little
headquarters in the uppermost residence—the very same
cell in which I bravely confronted Kornblatt mere days
ago. In the chaos of last night's technical malfunctions,
you're scared. You're confused. You're looking for a firm
hand on your shoulder, letting you know that everything's
going to be okay.

And I'm here to say, totally! Everything is under control. Madame J is here, of course, resplendent and calm
as ever. Chief Grunfeld is here, standing guard at the cell
door, silent as an elderly condor. A couple midlevel lackeys
are here—Undersecretary Moritz and some thin-armed

man named Bipple. And even yours truly; this is no time for ego, so please do not make a big deal when I inform you that I have been appointed Director of Alternative Narrative Formats for the special operational committee.

Yes, it's just the five of us—a lean, tight-knit group, streamlined for quick decisions and crisp action. Intimate, even. Five is maybe roughly three too many, if the goal is maximum efficiency and mind-meld and soul-communion, and sure, I may have been interrupted on the verge of a life-altering, heart-swelling, panty-melting proclamation—but right now what's important is establishing order and peace in the aftermath of last night's little blip of asymmetrical discord. And rest assured: we're on it. Up here in the Nerve Center, which is what we've been calling our new HQ, we're digging in and getting down to business. Committees have been established, along with the corresponding subcommittees and exchequers. All votes and motions are recorded in triplicate.

It's actually really nice up here. Cozy. I don't know what the prisoners were complaining about. And the cell window affords us a perfect vantage from which to monitor the situation below. It does *not* look pretty, let me tell you. People milling around, directionless, holding cups brimming with frothy beverages. Lots of balloons. The wafting aroma of tedfruit smoothies. It's a real mess, and on the ground it must be even worse.

Which is why we've deployed elite members of the Uniformed Youth to root out the instigators. There's one now—I watch him far below, stalking an unscrupulous fomenter. He moves through the crowd unnoticed, like a pointy finger penetrating a sponge cake, stalking his prey. Closer, now closer—even from up here I can see him squint as he locates his victim and leaps into action, walking briskly and now running toward . . . the cotton candy stand. Hmm. He buys several batonsful and walks back in the opposite direction, smiling widely, where he hands them out to—wait, are those the Veneron brothers, junior equestrian champions? Their tassels are in complete disarray, among other violations. Well, good—upheaval has a certain clarifying effect. I don't know why we didn't do this sooner, to be honest.

The elder Veneron now appears to be performing some sort of dance. He also appears to have removed his pants.

Anyway, long story short: Nothing to worry about. We got this. We'll wait right here, monitoring the situation until everyone realizes their mistake(s) and asks us to come down and kill the insurgents. At which point we'll *consider* their request. We're not even totally sure we want to continue ruling this place, to be honest. It's kind of a drag, all the complaining and gloom. No one ever says thank you. No one ever does anything for themselves.

"You're exactly right," said Chief Grunfeld, breaking his silent vigil. "Ungrateful, that's what they are."

Apparently I'd been saying all this out loud. Old newscaster's habit.

"I bet they can hardly even operate a scroller," sneered Bipple. "I'd like to see them try."

"I'd certainly rather see them try than *smell* them try," said Moritz, "if you know what I mean."

We all chuckled. It felt good to laugh. Though, to be honest, these other guys were kind of cluttering up the joint. It seemed to me that government proceedings might be more streamlined and generally comfortable if Madame J could have the quarters to herself, with me serving as a facilitator to convey her vision and edicts to the others, experienced as I am in the communicatory arts, which could enable a close working relationship, allowing for a deeper level of—

"Um, guys?" said Madame J. "Could someone hand me Simeon?"

I looked at Grunfeld. Grunfeld looked at Moritz. Moritz looked at Bipple. Bipple looked at me. Madame J peered absently out the narrow window, hand outstretched for the creature. Her fingers waggled expectantly.

"I believe that would fall under Mr. Moritz's departmental jurisdiction," said Bipple.

"Certainly not!" said Moritz. "Chief Grunfeld here has responsibility for all citizen monitoring and locational awareness."

"*Citizen* monitoring!" growled Grunfeld. "Simeon, though adorable, technically qualifies as a possession of the state, thereby subject to Bipple's oversight."

"A possession?" I said, disgusted. "Our beloved Simeon? A *possession*?"

Madame J snapped her fingers and held out her palm. "Will someone please just hand him to me?"

"His, well, his location is currently," said Grunfeld, "unestablished."

"Of course, we will quickly delegate full responsibility to the appropriate," said Bipple, "committee."

"It's just that, at the moment, we aren't entirely certain where Simeon," said Moritz, wincing, "is."

Madame J finally turned from the window and stared at us. It was, I believe, the first time we had ever truly locked eyes (not counting the various J holograms in my house, the gazes of which follow me as I perform my daily ablutions), and I felt myself go red in a number of places.

Her porcelain forehead wrinkled. "You're telling me Simeon is . . . lost?"

"Well," Moritz said, raising a finger to qualify her statement, then slowly dropped his hand back into the pocket of his fleecy vest.

"He's a fucking *octopus*, you dopes. He's goddamned *made* to stick to things. How could you possibly have lost him?"

"You must admit," Grunfeld whispered, "he was well trained. Athletic. And you know how smart they are, octopi?"

"Maybe he just stepped out for a smoothie?"

Bipple added. "I mean, they are very refreshing and, well, smooth?"

Madame J's features seemed to sort of shimmy, like they were about to shoot right off her face. "Well, I can see I'm up here with the best and brightest," she said, trembling. "Grunfeld, you can't even keep track of your own basic hygiene, let alone a rare motherfucking octopus that also happens to be your boss's personal companion and a symbol to free people everywhere. That's a bang-up résumé, you pus-bloated strip mall hag."

Moritz tittered nervously. "And you," Madame said, darting her eyes at the oblong man, "you've got the mental horsepower of an oven mitt. I wouldn't trust you with my dingleberry collection." She turned to Bipple. "I don't even know what that guy's name is. And you," she said, talking to me! "You're six feet of pistol-whip bait. Quit thumbing your fucking scroll-wang and do anything fucking useful, like finding my fucking pet or drowning yourself in your own swamp diarrhea." She kicked a slop bucket toward me. Toward *me*. A ropey green strand of something sloshed onto my knee. I looked at it for a long time, trying hard to convince myself it wasn't in the shape of a heart.

"Oh, sweet Jesu," Madame said, collapsing on the wooden plank that serves as our break room, just until we get some better stuff in here. "I am truly frangled now. Deep in the bung pit. Eating foie gras with a baby spoon. They're out there, doing whatever in the sweet living hell that they want, and I'm trapped in here with you incompetent porklings. Kill me now, please, please." She buried her face in her hands and leaned against the stone wall.

There was a long silence. Grunfeld opened his mouth and then closed it. Moritz and Bipple shuffled their feet awkwardly. I tried to stay calm and maintain my composure, although inside I was beaming. "Find my fucking pet," she'd said to me. "Do anything fucking useful." To me and no one else. *Do anything fucking useful.* It looped through my brain until the words were more music than language. She wanted me to be useful! And I was ready to be used. I'll find her fucking pet, for sure. And then I'll do the next thing she asks of me, and the thing after that. And each time I complete a task, she'll look at me and in her mind she'll wonder how she ever got along without me. And we'll keep going like that, with me blowing her mind and her having her mind blown, on and on until we're ruling this place again. I mean, until she's ruling the place, and I'm standing by her side, giving unconditional support and back rubs.

Down in the Termination Field, citizens now appear to be using the Slow Squisher as a moonbounce. They are smiling and bouncing, while others throw what appears to be popcorn, which the bouncers attempt to catch in their mouths.

Well, no one can bounce forever, right? Soon they'll realize what a hassle it is—not just the bouncing, but all that responsibility, all those decisions. They'll find that freedom, at the end of the day, is just a brown, farty, toxic cloud that makes everything a hundred times harder than it needs to be. And then they'll come begging for us to take the reins again, and the two of us will birth a new nation of wriggling joy.

It's just a matter of time. We'll wait right here.

SOURCE CITIZEN
[Flora Bialy]

RANK
[0001]

RECIPE NAME
[   ]

INGREDIENTS
[   ]

INSTRUCTIONS

That night was a joyous, blurry mess, an endless procession of musicians and jugglers and acrobats and . . . well,
often I wasn't entirely sure *what* the act was. But there
was always another, and another, and another, pushing
their way toward the front of the stage, where years of
pent-up fear and gloom came rushing out through their
spontaneous displays of secret talent. It was hard to tell
whether some of them were even any good—actually, it
was easy to tell that most of them were quite bad—but
quality, that night, felt irrelevant, outdated.

They seemed to assume I was somehow in charge,
and I didn't want to disappoint. Each new performer
would emerge from the crowd, beckon me close, and then

whisper what they had to offer. It went on and on like this, act after act. An elderly man, teetering on his cane, hobbled up to me and put his hand on my shoulder. "When I crack my knuckles," he murmured, "it's quite loud."

"Your knuckles? They're . . . loud?" I whispered back.

"Really quite loud, yes."

"Okay," I said. "Okay!" I stepped to the front of the stage. "Ladies and gentlemen," I boomed, "please cover your ears and clench your bowels, because the Knuckle Cruncher is here, and he's looking to crunch a whole bunch. So, without further ado . . ." and so on.

The crunching was, in fact, very loud.

People lined up to my left, did their thing, and then filed off to the right to rejoin the hooting audience. I had lost my cohorts in the happy masses, until I turned and saw Dieter next in line, fidgeting nervously. He came toward me and whispered, "Um, lonely man, eating, you know . . . corn." My heart sank. "Lonely Man Eating Corn" was perhaps Dieter's least popular, most rage-inducing bit. (One night Mrs. Tralm actually gave up her wheelchair so that her sons could hurl it at Dieter, hence the wheelchair-shaped scar across his back.) But the crowd was already applauding eagerly, the poor fools, so I turned forward and bellowed, "Mere words cannot contain the pathos herein, so I daren't even try. Please welcome the Sculptor of Silence, the Master of Mum, a man who will haunt your dreams and render your waking life a cheap fraud—Dieter Brakconner!"

Dieter dragged a large wooden table behind him and set it down at the center of the stage. The crowd hushed as he lit an imaginary stove and filled an imaginary pot. Dieter labored over every step—boiling the "water," shucking the "ear," blowing on the "hot" "corn." I couldn't even watch the meticulous, mournful buttering interlude. When his meal was finally finished, he brandished an invisible napkin and wiped his mouth clean. He patted his forehead, placed the napkin back on the table, and took a deep bow.

I rushed back onstage. "Dieter Brakconner, everybody, testing out some new material," I said, hoping to spirit him off before the tedfruits began flying.

The applause was deafening.

Dieter bowed once more, and beamed, and bowed, and the ovation continued. He lifted the heavy wooden table over his head like a trophy, and the applause went even louder. He smiled proudly and then snapped the table in half over his knee, and the arena shuddered with stomping feet.

Faces appeared at the narrow windows of the tower—longtime prisoners, hesitantly peering down at the celebration. "Come on down, come on down!" we chanted. But the pale faces remained fixed at the windows. "Oh, look here, I have the keys!" shouted a guard, who had evidently drunk a great deal of tedwine and was swirling his many tassels into a kind of inverted beehive. The guard stumbled into the needle and we watched as, one by one, the faces of the prisoners disappeared from their windows and reap-peared at the tower's front gate. Each time one emerged, a family would rush forward for a round of tearful bear hugs, and the joyous spectators sighed with delight.

Onstage, Bruce and Sharon were juggling a wedding cake, a kitten, and an old poncho, eating a bite of cake between each throw. For the finale, they nibbled all the way to the center of the cake . . . revealing Kovacsz hiding inside, which wasn't even physically comprehensible. He burst through the yellow sponge cake and took a triumphant, icing-covered bow, somehow also wearing the poncho and snuggling the kitten. It was very confusing, but impressive nevertheless.

Off to the right I saw Reuben, surrounded by a gaggle of little girls who were braiding his beard into psychedelic whorls. Valentino and Martin shared a smoothie as they watched the young cosmetologists work their magic.

I searched the yard for Marina. She stood alone near the entrance to our old immolation hut, clapping politely amid the chaotic revelry. I started to thread my way toward her when I saw her freeze. The black hilt of a dagger was stuck in the wall just inches from her neck. Four more hilts appeared a moment later, delicately outlining her skull. From out of the crowd emerged the black-clad prong thrower. He approached Marina and bowed, extending his hand. She smiled, reached out her own, and they disappeared into the throng.

Dawn approached and the stage was finally empty,

but nobody seemed ready to go home. It was as if the whole night might have been nothing but a dream, and we were all afraid to wake up. Real or not, I had one last act to introduce before we could leave. I saw his silhouette near the edge of the crowd, leaning against the bone witherer. I stepped back into the spotlight at the center of the stage.

"Citizens, friends, handsome people of Destina. This day has given you wonders, thrills, delights. But let us not forget our star attraction, the man who brought us all together, villain to a nation, inspiration to a few, master of all rings—ladies and gentlemen, I present to you: Zloty Kornblatt!"

I swept my arm toward Zloty, and the crowd parted smoothly. He blinked once or twice, then noticed the pool of light surrounding him. He walked slowly to the stage. The audience was so quiet that you could hear Mrs. Tralm's lung machine. Kovacsz, Marina, Reuben, and the rest all stood in the front row, hands clasped. Zloty paused, bowed his head, and began.

It was, of course, his reenactment of the life of the herpetologist Etienne Stratford-Hicks. The early years of garter snakes and creek newts. The teenage journeys through Africa and Siam. The dental school detour. The passionate love affair with Assata Boumedienne, infamous psychobotanist. The later years, establishing bylaws and membership policies for the East Anglian Reptilian Society.

The crowd was rapt. Even the campfires seemed to perk up and flicker toward the stage. Even the locusts paused their carnal screeches and craned their antennae.

Zloty didn't fall down once.

It actually wasn't too bad.

And after Stratford-Hicks's poignant deathbed farewell, the pillowcases somehow contorting into a surreal kickline of origami iguanas, Zloty stood tall, closed his eyes, and took a deep, deep bow. All I could see was his battered hat, his scuffed shoes, and his wide outstretched arms. He was free, and we had freed him. Everything would be different now.

There was a long hush—and then the tedfruits began to fly. Not just tedfruits, but also cornroasters, whipfish crackles, snumgum snacksticks; the entire concessions inventory, it seemed, had been repurposed to accompany the boos that were now raining down upon Zloty.

He smiled at the masses and bowed again, his tuxedo turning orange with spattered pulp. Dieter scurried onstage and scooped Zloty under one arm, and together we ran home to Burford.

ACKNOWLEDGMENTS

Russell Quinn, Matt Derby, Rachel Khong,
Adam Levin, Kevin Moffett, Colin Winnette,
Sean McDonald, Nora Barlow, Dan Schofield,
Sam Riley, Michelle Quint, Jory John,
Richard Parks, Walter Green.

A NOTE ABOUT THE ARTIST

Ian Huebert is a printmaker and an illustrator. He enjoys
making things by hand, and more often than not these
things end up in books. He is working on an MFA
at the University of Iowa Center for the Book.

For more news, snacks, and citizenship,
enter the Index:
www.thepickleindex.com